The wall of people shifted and suddenly, Sarina was there.

Sarina. *Here.*

Matteo went still. Except, for once it wasn't ice that held him in its grip. It was much too hot for that. Too electric.

Because she was *right here*, and this was why he had come, he acknowledged now. He had put himself in her city as if it was a test of fate—and he'd won.

His gaze, greedy to take in all of her after all these weeks, stopped short at her belly.

And the last time he'd seen her belly, it had been flat. Not jutting out as it was now in a dress she'd clearly worn to emphasize its roundness.

It was as if a bomb detonated inside Matteo. He was shocked to realize that he remained in one piece.

One moment he was a man who traveled the world, carrying his ghosts within him in and out of hotels and offices, one bleeding into the next while he remained numb.

And in the next, he was alive.

One Night With Consequences

When one night...leads to pregnancy!

When succumbing to a night of unbridled desire, it's impossible to think past the morning after!

But with the sheets barely settled, that little blue line appears on the pregnancy test, and it doesn't take long to realize that one night of white-hot passion has turned into a lifetime of consequences!

Only one question remains:

How do you tell a man you've just met that you're about to share more than just his bed?

Find out in:

The Innocent's Shock Pregnancy by Carol Marinelli

An Innocent, A Seduction, A Secret by Abby Green

Carrying the Sheikh's Baby by Heidi Rice

The Venetian One-Night Baby by Melanie Milburne

Heiress's Pregnancy Scandal by Julia James

Innocent's Nine-Month Scandal by Dani Collins

Look for more One Night With Consequences coming soon!

Caitlin Crews

———

THE ITALIAN'S TWIN
CONSEQUENCES

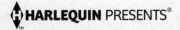 HARLEQUIN PRESENTS®

Recycling programs
for this product may
not exist in your area.

ISBN-13: 978-1-335-47827-6

The Italian's Twin Consequences

First North American publication 2019

This edition published by arrangement with Harlequin Books S.A.

For questions and comments about the quality of this book, please contact us at CustomerService@Harlequin.com.

Printed in U.S.A.

www.Harlequin.com

USA TODAY bestselling and RITA® Award–nominated author **Caitlin Crews** loves writing romance. She teaches her favorite romance novels in creative-writing classes at places like UCLA Extension's prestigious Writers' Program, where she finally gets to utilize the MA and PhD in English literature she received from the University of York in England. She currently lives in the Pacific Northwest with her very own hero and too many pets. Visit her at caitlincrews.com.

Books by Caitlin Crews

Harlequin Presents

Undone by the Billionaire Duke

Conveniently Wed!

Imprisoned by the Greek's Ring
My Bought Virgin Wife

One Night With Consequences

A Baby to Bind His Bride

Bound to the Desert King

Sheikh's Secret Love-Child

Scandalous Royal Brides

The Prince's Nine-Month Scandal
The Billionaire's Secret Princess

Stolen Brides

The Bride's Baby of Shame

Visit the Author Profile page
at Harlequin.com for more titles.

To Maisey, who likes to sit in coffeehouses
and ask me *what if...?*

CHAPTER ONE

"I'M AWARE THE terms of these sessions were set out in writing and forwarded to you by your board of directors, Mr. Combe, but I think it's useful to go over them again in person. While you and I will be doing the talking, I must stress that you are not my client. I will be presenting my findings to the board rather than exploring therapeutic solutions with you. Do you understand what that means?"

Matteo Combe stared at the woman seated across from him in the ancient library of the Venetian villa that had been in his mother's family since the dawn of time, or thereabouts. The San Giacomos were aristocratic and noble, with blood so blue it sang its own aria. They could even claim a smattering of Italian princes, Matteo's great-grandfather among them. That he had not passed along his title had been, as far as Matteo was aware, the greatest disappointment of his grandfather's life.

It would be a spot of luck indeed if Matteo could

concern himself with such disappointments. Instead, he had to handle more pressing concerns at the moment, such as the preservation of the family business that his father's decidedly working-class forebears had built from nothing in the north of England during the Industrial Revolution. That he was choosing to handle that situation here in this self-congratulatory aristocratic villa was for his own private satisfaction.

And perhaps he'd thought he might cow the woman—the psychiatrist—sitting with him while he was at it.

Dr. Sarina Fellows was, by his reckoning, the first American to set foot on the premises. Ever. Matteo was vaguely surprised the whole of the villa hadn't sunk into the Grand Canal in genteel protest the moment she'd set foot on the premises.

But then, villas in Venice were as renowned for their remarkable tenacity in the face of adverse conditions as he was.

Sarina looked as brisk and efficient as her words had been, which boded ill. She was dressed entirely in funereal black, but was saved from dourness by the quiet excellence of the pieces she wore. Matteo knew artisanal Italian design when he saw it. Her hair was a dark black silk, bound up in a crisp chignon at the nape of her neck. Her eyes were a complicated brown shot through with amber, the irises ringed in black. And her lips were pure perfection, begging for a man to taste them, for all that, she had left them bare of any color.

She looked like what she was, he supposed. The agent of his destruction, if his enemies had their way.

Matteo had no intention of allowing anything to destroy him. Not this woman. Not his parents' unexpected deaths within weeks of each other, leaving nothing in their wake but the fallout of the secrets they'd kept—and Matteo as the unwilling executor of the things they'd hidden while they lived. Not even his younger sister's unfortunate life choices, which had led Matteo straight here, where the chairman of Combe Industries' board—his late father's best friend—now wished to take control.

Nothing would destroy him. Matteo wouldn't allow it.

But he had to tolerate this farcical exercise first.

Sarina aimed what he suspected was meant to be a sympathetic smile his way. It struck him as rather more challenging instead. And Matteo had never been one to back down from a challenge— especially when he really should have, to keep the peace.

Lord, but he detested this process already. And it had only just begun.

He recalled that she'd asked him a question. And he'd agreed, hadn't he? He'd given his word. He would sit here and subject himself to this intrusion and he would, yes, answer her questions. Each and every one.

Through gritted teeth, if necessary.

"I'm perfectly aware of why you are here, Miss Fellows," he managed to reply. What he did not manage to do was strip his voice of impatience. Frustration. And what his erstwhile personal assistant often dared to categorize, to his face, as sheer orneriness.

"Doctor."

He didn't follow. "Excuse me?"

Her smile was all sharp edges. "It's *Dr.* Fellows, Mr. Combe. Not *Miss* Fellows. I hope that critical distinction assures you that these conversations, while perhaps difficult, are wholly professional."

"I'm delighted to hear it," he said, wondering if he'd done that deliberately. He'd always prided himself on being far less of a blunt instrument than his father, renowned far and wide for his bluster and the sucker punch to back it up. But then, he'd never been in a situation like this before. "I have not spent much time—or any time, if I am honest—in mandated therapy, but the professional nature of this experience was, of course, my foremost concern."

The late spring storm beat against the windows outside, rushing in from the lagoon and threatening to flood the Piazza San Marco the way it did more commonly in fall and winter. The threat of high water reflected Matteo's mood perfectly. But the woman across from him only aimed that same smile at him as the rain slapped against the glass, wholly undeterred.

"I understand that there is resistance to this kind of therapy. Or indeed, any kind of therapy. Perhaps it will be helpful to dive in straightaway." She settled there in the high-backed, antique chair that he knew for a fact was excruciatingly uncomfortable as if it had been crafted to her precise ergonomic specifications. She made a show of checking her notes in the sleek leather folder she brandished before her like a weapon. "You are the president and CEO of Combe Industries, correct?"

Matteo had dressed casually for this interview. Or *session*, as the woman had insisted upon calling it. Now he wished he hadn't. He would have greatly preferred the comfort of one of his bespoke suits, the better to remind himself that he wasn't simply any old ruffian in off the street. He was Matteo Combe, raised to be the eldest son and reluctant heir to the San Giacomo fortune and the sprawling, multinational corporation that his father's gritty, determined Combe ancestors had built from nothing long ago in the stark mill towns of northern England.

You need to humanize yourself, his assistant had insisted.

That was the trouble, of course. Matteo had

never been very good at being human. With his family—his careless, scandalous mother and his bullish, jealous father and all their theatrics—he'd never had much practice.

He forced a smile now. Something else he didn't have much practice with. "I was president of the corporation before my father's death. He had been grooming me to take his place for some time." Since birth, in fact, though he kept that to himself. "I became CEO after he passed."

"And you chose to mark the occasion of his passing by descending into a physical altercation with one of the funeral guests. A prince, no less."

The smile on his mouth felt strained. "I wasn't concerned with what he was at the time. All I knew was that he was the one who impregnated and abandoned my sister."

Sarina checked her notes again, rustling through her papers in an officious manner that put Matteo's teeth on edge. Or *more* on edge.

"You're referring to your sister, Pia, who is some years younger than you, but is, in point of fact, an adult woman. Capable of choosing to bear a child if she so wishes, presumably."

Matteo eyed the woman sitting across from him in that draconian chair his grandfather had made him sit in when the old man felt Matteo needed to learn humility. He'd had a dossier prepared on her, of course. Sarina Fellows had been born and raised in San Francisco and had distinguished herself in one of the city's foremost private academies. She'd gone on to Berkeley, then Stanford, and instead of going into private practice as a psychiatrist, had opened up her own consulting firm instead. Now she traveled the globe, working most closely with corporations on various projects where psychological profiles on executives were needed.

Matteo was simply her latest victim.

Because he hadn't simply punched out the jack-ass prince who'd left Pia pregnant and alone, which he still wasn't the least bit sorry about. His little sister was the only family member Matteo had ever had that he could say he adored unreservedly, if often from afar, as the heiress to two grand fortunes was something of a target. For unscrupulous fortune hunters as well as princes, apparently. He'd happily do it again, and worse. But he'd done it in full view of the paparazzi, who'd had a field day.

Chip off the old block, they'd called him in a frenzy of malicious glee. They'd dragged his late father's many scandals and altercations back into the light of day, in case anyone had been tempted to forget who Eddie Combe had been, mere days after his death. It had taken a single snide news cycle for the vicious tabloids to start speculating about whether or not Matteo was the right person to run his own damned company.

He'd had no choice but to submit to the demands

of his prissy, pearl-clutching board of directors, all of whom had fluttered about claiming they'd never seen such behavior in all their days. A bald-faced lie, since they'd all gotten their positions in the first place from Eddie, who'd been a brawler by nature and inclination.

But Eddie was dead, which Matteo still found difficult to believe. All that force and power and fury, gone. And Matteo had to get high marks from the good doctor after the way he'd channeled his father at the funeral, or risk a vote of no confidence.

Matteo could have quashed the motion outright. But he knew that the company was in a time of transition. If he wanted to lead—instead of what his father had done all this time, which was bully, threaten, lie and occasionally cheat—he had to start off on the right foot.

Especially when he knew exactly what other revelations awaited in his parents' wills.

"My sister is naive and trusting," Matteo said shortly. "She was raised to know very little of the world, much less the nature of men. I'm afraid I don't take kindly to those who would take advantage of her better nature."

Sarina shifted slightly in the seat opposite, staring at him as if he was some kind of science experiment.

It was not the way women normally looked at

him and Matteo couldn't say he liked it much. Especially when he couldn't help but notice the doctor was not exactly hard on the eyes. Her legs were slim and toned, and it was entirely too tempting to picture them draped over his shoulders as he drove into her—

Focus, he ordered himself.

He knew too much about her to imagine she would take kindly to his line of thought. He knew that she had built her consulting business out of nothing and was ruthless, driven—qualities he possessed himself and usually appreciated in others. Though not, perhaps, in this particular scenario, when all of that knife-edged ferocity was directed at him.

"You look as if you've seen a ghost," she said, almost idly. He knew better than to imagine anything about her was the least bit *idle.* "Have you?"

"There are ghosts everywhere in a house like this," Matteo replied, unsettled despite himself. Not at the notion of ghosts. But at the strange sensation that had washed over him at the suggestion of them—the idea that he'd met this woman before when he knew he hadn't. He shoved the odd sense of recognition aside. "The halls are cluttered with my ancestors. I'm sure some of them enjoy a good haunting, but I can't say they've ever bothered me. Feel free to sleep here tonight and see if you receive a ghostly visitation."

"That would be something indeed, as I don't believe in ghosts." Her head tilted to one side. "Do you?"

"If I did, I'd be unlikely to mention it. I wouldn't wish to fail your test."

"This isn't a test, Mr. Combe. These are conversations, nothing more. And surely you understand why your shareholders and directors take a dim view of the sort of violent, antisocial behavior you displayed at the funeral."

He lifted a shoulder and then dropped it, affecting a carelessness he had never actually felt. "I was protecting my sister."

"Walk me through your thought process, if you will." Sarina propped one elbow on the arm of the chair, then tapped one of her long, elegant fingers against her jaw. He shouldn't have been mesmerized by the motion. "Your sister is six months pregnant. And not, by all reports, incapacitated in any way. My research into Pia indicates she's a well-educated, well-traveled, perfectly independent woman. Yet you felt some archaic need to leap to her defense. In a markedly brutal fashion."

"I am distressingly archaic." Matteo wasn't sure why that word ignited like a flame in him. Or maybe that was just her fingers on her own jaw, making him wish it was his hand instead. "It's a natural consequence of having been raised in a historic family, I suspect."

"All families are historic, Mr. Combe. By definition. It's called *generations*. It's just so rarely *your* history, complete with Venetian villas and claims of nobility." He thought he saw something flash in her gaze then, but she repressed it in the next moment. "But back to your sister. Did you imagine you were defending her honor? How... patriarchal."

He didn't like the way she said that word, biting off the syllables as if they were weapons. "I apologize for loving my sister."

Matteo loved Pia, certainly, though he couldn't say he understood her. Or her choices when she must have known the whole of the world would be watching her—but then, perhaps she hadn't had that pounded into her head from a young age the way he had.

"*Love* is a very interesting word to use in these circumstances, I think," Sarina said. "I'm not certain how I would feel if my brother chose to express his so-called love for me by planting his fist into the face of the father of my unborn child."

"Do you have a brother?"

He knew she didn't. Sarina Fellows was the only child of a British linguistics professor and his Japanese biochemist wife, who had met in graduate school in London and ended up in California together, teaching at the same university.

"I don't have a brother," she replied, seemingly

unfazed that he'd caught her out. "But I was raised by people who prize nonviolence. Unlike you, if I'm understanding your family's rather checkered past correctly."

He could have asked her which checkered past she meant. The San Giacomos had dueled and schemed throughout the ages. The Combes had been more direct, and significantly more likely to throw a punch. But it was checkered all around, anyway he looked at it.

"If I'm guilty of anything, it's being an over-zealous older brother," Matteo said. And then remembered—the way he kept doing, with the same mix of shock and something a great deal like regret—that he too had an older brother. An older brother his mother had given up when she was a teenager, yet had dropped into her will like a bomb. An older brother Matteo had yet to meet and still couldn't quite believe was real.

Maybe that was why he'd done nothing about it. Yet.

He tried to flash another smile.

Not that it was any use. The doctor didn't change expression at all. Instead, she sat there in silence, until his smile faded away.

He understood it was a tactic. A strategy, nothing more. It was one he had employed a thousand times himself. But he certainly didn't like it being aimed his way.

He felt the urge, as everyone always did, to fill the silence. He refrained.

Instead, he settled there in the ancient armchair where he remembered his own grandfather sitting decades ago, shrouded in bitterness because he was noble, yet not royal. Matteo lounged there the way he remembered the old man had, endeavoring to look as unbothered as he ought to have been. Because this was a minor inconvenience, surely. An impertinence, nothing more.

He was submitting to this because he chose to. Because it was an olive branch he could wave at his board to prove that he was both conscientious and different from his father. Not because he *had* to.

It didn't matter if the doctor didn't realize that.

Besides, the longer she stared at him, letting the silence stretch and thicken between them, the more he found it impossible to think about anything but how distractingly attractive she was. He'd expected someone far more like a battle-ax. Fussy and of advanced years, for example.

He suspected her beauty was another tactic.

Because Sarina Fellows didn't look at all like the kind of woman who could hold such supposed power over his life. She looked a great deal more like the sort of woman he liked to take to his bed. Sleek and elegant. Poised. Matteo preferred them intelligent and pedigreed, because he liked clever conversation as well as greedier, more sensual pastimes.

If she hadn't been sent here to judge him, he might have amused himself by finding ways to get his hands up beneath the hem of the elegant pencil skirt she wore and—

"Toxic masculinity," she pronounced, with something like satisfaction in her tone.

Matteo blinked. "Is that a diagnosis?"

"The good news, Mr. Combe, is that you are hardly unique." It was definitely satisfaction. Her dark eyes gleamed. "You seem unrepentant, and think about what we're discussing here. A funeral is generally held to be a gathering where the bereaved can say their final goodbyes to a lost loved one. You chose to make it a boxing ring. And you also took it upon yourself to draw blood, terrify those around you, and humiliate the sister you claim to love, all to assuage *your* sense of fractured honor."

He didn't sigh at that, though it took an act of will. "You obviously never met my father. There were no bereaved at his funeral and furthermore, he would have been the first to cheer on a spot of boxing."

"I find that difficult to believe. And, frankly, more evidence of the kind of cowboy inappropriateness that seems to be part and parcel of the Matteo Combe package."

"I am Italian on one side and British on the other, Dr. Fellows. There is no part of me that is a cowboy. In any respect."

"I'm using the term to illustrate a strain of toxic male vigilantism that, as far as I'm aware, you haven't bothered to apologize for. Then or now."

"If I felt the need to apologize for defending my sister's honor, which I do not, that would be a discussion I had with Pia," Matteo said quietly. "Not with you. Certainly not with my board. Nor, for that matter, with the clamoring public."

Her pen was poised over her paper. "So you do feel remorse for your brutality? Or you don't?"

What Matteo felt like doing would, he suspected, inspire her to call him names far worse than *cowboy*. He spread his hands out in front of him, as if in some kind of surrender. When he didn't have the slightest idea how to surrender. To anything or anyone.

"Remorse is a lot like guilt. Or shame. Both useless emotions that have more to do with others than with the self." He dropped his hands. "I cannot change the past. Even if I wanted to."

"How convenient. And since you can't change it, why bother discussing it. Is that your policy?"

"I cannot say that I have a policy. As I have never subjected myself to these, quote-unquote, 'conversations' before."

"Somehow I am unshocked."

"But I am here now, am I not? I have promised to answer any question you might have. We can talk at length on any topic you desire. I am nothing if not compliant." He made himself smile again, though it felt like a blade. "And toxic, apparently."

"*Compliant* is an interesting word choice," Sarina said, and he was sure there was laughter in her voice, though he could see no sign of it anywhere on her face. "Do you think it's an adequate word to describe you or your behavior?"

"I have opened my home. I have invited you into it and lo, you came. I have agreed to have as many of these conversations as you deem necessary. And for this, I am called *toxic* instead of *accommodating*."

"That word bothers you."

"I would not say that it bothers me." What bothered him was the pointlessness of this. The waste of his time and energy. And yes, the fact that she was distractingly beautiful—which, he had to remind himself, was nothing but another weapon. "But it is not as if one wishes to be called toxic, is it? It is certainly not a compliment."

"And you are a man who is accustomed to compliments, is that it?"

He knew better, but still, he felt his mouth curve. "It will perhaps shock you to learn that most women who make my acquaintance do not find me the least bit toxic."

"Are you attempting to make this session sexual, Mr. Combe?" He saw her eyes flash at that and he could have sworn what he saw in them then was triumph. It told him he was in deeper trouble than he'd thought even before she smirked. "Oh dear. This is much worse than I thought."

CHAPTER TWO

MATTEO COMBE WAS precisely the kind of wealthy, pompous, arrogant man of too much undeserved power Sarina Fellows hated most.

He was remarkably handsome, which to her mind was a very serious strike against him, right from the start. His was the kind of attractiveness that made people silly when they encountered it. It was the walk into walls, trip over your own two feet, start giggling like a twelve-year-old sort of silliness, and it appalled her deeply that she could feel the swell of that reaction inside of her when she'd long considered herself immune to his type.

But he was different, somehow. He was…*more*. It was something about the glossiness of his dark hair, the assertive line of his jaw. It was his aristocratic nose and those gray eyes like a storm. It was something about the seething confidence he wore like a kind of cloak, draped about his athletic, rangy body and making it very clear that he was succumbing to her—to this evaluation his own board had demanded—because he chose to do so. That no force on earth could compel him to do a single thing he didn't wish to do.

He reminded her of a mighty river, roaring over a great ledge. Powerful. Kinetic and dynamic.

Dangerous, something in her whispered.

Sarina dismissed that almost as soon as the word formed inside her. He was beautiful, yes. Somehow austere and lush at once, with that face of his. And he was rich. Filthily, vomitously wealthy. One branch of his family tree was stuck deep into the Yorkshire mills, hardy and tough, inside and out. The other stretched back into the golden age of the Italian Renaissance, which was right about the time this particular villa had been built.

Sarina understood exactly why he had insisted their first meeting be here, in the living fairy tale that was Venice. He wanted her to come all the way into this city of sighs and ancient palazzos and history like a bright tapestry in which his family was a shining, golden thread, the better to gasp and flutter over all his wealth and consequence.

Except Sarina wasn't the fluttering kind.

And Matteo Combe had no idea what he was in for.

It wasn't only that Sarina hated men like him, though she did. It was that she knew them. She knew what they were capable of, certainly, and she'd developed an acute allergy to their form of arrogance. The best friend she'd had since childhood, who she'd considered her sister, had succumbed to an addiction to a man just like Matteo. Rashly confident, propped up on all that history and the money acquired for him across centuries, and catered to by everyone he had ever met, every single day for the whole of his life.

Oh yes. Sarina knew all about men like him.

Sarina didn't need to destroy him, necessarily. But she thought of men like Matteo as big, blown-up balloons, and as it happened, she'd set herself up to be the perfect, pointed pin. She'd been popping overweening male egos professionally now long enough to have quite the reputation for taking masters of the universe down a few pegs, to the mortal men of questionable moral character they usually were beneath all the bluster.

Some of the men she was called in to consult with were decent. In the absence of a record of misdeeds and bad behavior, she was more than happy to issue a glowing report on the man in question. She didn't hate men, as many had accused her. She hated *bad* men who abused their power and those vulnerable to it.

She felt sure that Jeanette, wherever she was now, was looking down on her in support.

And the fact that the particular rich, arrogant man in front of her had already managed to worm his way beneath her skin in a way the others never had? With all that dark and brooding *certainty* he exuded like a rich scent?

Well. That was between her and the private conversations she had in her own head. She had no intention of letting him see it.

"You want me to have remorse," Matteo was saying. He was sitting in an armchair Sarina didn't have to know anything about antiques to know was exquisite and priceless, looking entirely too much like a king for her peace of mind. "If I cannot produce any on cue, does that mean I fail this examination?"

"This isn't a pass or fail experience." She jotted down a few words on the pad in front of her, more to make him uncomfortable than to record anything. "Do you find that unnerving?"

"That my future is in the hands of someone who cannot answer a direct question?" His gray eyes gleamed. "Not in the least."

She hadn't expected him to be dry. And all the pictures in the world—Sarina was fairly certain she'd viewed every last one of them, purely for research purposes—didn't do justice to the particular wild darkness that was Matteo Combe. It was that thick, near-black hair of his, edging toward the border of unruly. It was the slate gray of his gaze that made her think not only of rain, but more worryingly, of dancing in it.

Even when she knew full well that way lay madness. And things much worse that a little madness.

He usually dressed in expensive business suits and sleek formal wear, the better to lord it over everyone else. But today he'd chosen to greet her in what she assumed passed for casual wear to a man like him. A pair of jeans that looked expensively frayed, because he'd obviously bought them that way. Men like Matteo didn't do anything that might lead to whitened knees or artful tears in denim, designer or not. His boots were very clearly handcrafted right here in Italy. And he sported the kind of T-shirt that had about as much in common with a run-of-the-mill cotton T-shirt from the stores regular people frequented as stealth fighter jets did with paper airplanes. Worse, the T-shirt clung to his torso, telling her things she didn't want to know about the extraordinary physical shape Matteo kept himself in.

She knew it already. She knew he liked to run miles upon miles. She knew he enjoyed epic swims and then, with his leftover energy and time, a great deal of flinging weights around. She'd read all of that, but it was one thing to *read* in a far-off hotel room. It was something else again to sit in the presence of a man who clearly preferred to use every iota of power he could, including the physical.

But she was here to assess his mental state, not gaze adoringly at the place where his bicep strained the hem of his T-shirt, so she frowned a little as she focused on him again.

"This will only be an adversarial relationship if you make it that way."

"It's an inherently adversarial relationship," he corrected her, mildly enough, though there was nothing mild in the way he gazed at her. "I suspect you know that."

"But you enjoy adversity in your relationships, don't you?"

He let out a laugh, as if she'd surprised him.

"I would not say that I *like* adversarial relationships. But in my family, there is almost no other kind."

"Yet you sat right there and told me how much you love your sister. Or do you consider love another form of adversity?"

"Your family is obviously different from mine or you would know the answer to that question."

Sarina knew entirely too much about his family, as did everyone else in the known world, because both branches of it had spent so much time dominating tabloid headlines. Even if she'd never looked one of them up deliberately, there would have been no avoiding them. Matteo's father had regularly appeared in the headlines, for this or that supposed marital or corporate indiscretion. His mother, meanwhile, had been widely held to be the most beautiful woman on the planet while she'd lived. Which had come with its own share of scandals and speculation, and all the attendant tabloid attention.

He and his sister were close, or so it was believed—or as close as they could be with a ten-year age gap between them, leaving Matteo as something more like a secondary parent than a brother.

In contrast, Sarina had been raised by chilly academics. They were far more concerned with their own research, their endless pursuit of publication, and the petty intellectual squabbles of their peers than the daughter she thought they'd had as an experiment in humanity more than any desire to parent. And they had less than no interest in any scandals she might have kicked up along the way.

Sarina couldn't imagine growing up in a place like this villa, no matter how lovely Venice was. She and Jeannette had grown up in side-by-side old houses in the Berkeley Hills, racing in and out of rooms notable for their towering piles of books and comfortable, threadbare rugs, muddy porches and overgrown yards. This villa was a dramatic clutter of perfectly preserved tapestries and heavy stone statues, slung about this chamber and that, lest anyone be tempted to forget that this was the very heart of old-world wealth.

She knew why he'd brought her here, but it was backfiring in ways she doubted he'd imagined. Because now she knew how seriously he took himself and his pedigree. And that could only work to her advantage.

"Why did you think that it was better to meet here?" she asked, keeping her voice cool. "In a place that is very clearly a home, and not part of your business empire? Is this another attempt on your part to steer our interactions toward something sexual?"

"You are the one who keeps mentioning sex, Dr. Fellows," Matteo said silkily. "Not me."

Somehow she kept any reaction to that off her face. "Yet you insisted we start here, not in one of your many offices. Can you explain that choice?"

"This is where I happen to be at the moment," he replied, and there was a certain smokiness in that voice of his with its unique accent, not quite British and not yet Italian. Something dark, and more compelling than she wanted to admit. To her horror, she felt a certain...*thrill* work its way through her, settling between her legs and worse, pulsing. She was so horrified she froze. "Both you and the chairman of my board impressed upon me that these meetings had to begin as soon as possible. Obedient in all things, I immediately made myself available."

There wasn't a single obedient thing about this man. Sarina ordered herself to concentrate on her reasons for being here and not that *pulsing* thing. Or the wildness she could sense in him, simmering there beneath his aristocratic surface.

"What I think, Mr. Combe, is that you wanted me to see this villa You wanted to impress me."

"I cannot imagine anything less on my mind than a desire to impress you."

"I'm assessing you for corporate reasons, yet you appear in a T-shirt. Here in this very personal space. At the very least, you aren't taking this seriously. Do you think that's wise?"

Something changed in his gaze then. Some flash of awareness, or temper. He leaned forward, resting his elbows on his knees, and she was suddenly aware of the fact that though he'd called it a library, this was really nothing more than a small living room. It just happened to contain a number of books. A fireplace. What had seemed like a reasonable amount of space without it feeling like a closet.

But when he shifted like that, he seemed to take up the whole of it.

"I would ordinarily spare a visitor a dreary history lesson, but there is very little personal about this villa. It appears as it always has. It is my job to be its steward, not a resident in any real sense. I must hand the villa on to the next generation intact. As it has been handed down, eldest son to eldest son, since the day it was built. For me, Doctor, there is no distinction between what is corporate and what is personal. My mother was a San Giacomo. Surely you must know what that means."

"Is this your way of reminding me that you're famous, Mr. Combe?"

"My family is not famous," he said gently. "Fame is the stuff of a moment, here and gone. My family—both of my families—are prominent and of significant means. And have been for some centuries."

"Do you think—"

"Let us cut to the chase, please." He interrupted her smoothly, but she was sure that was impatience she could see in his face. And his *please* wasn't any sort of supplication. "What is it you are looking for from me? Is it a certain set of words, arranged in a specific way, so as to assuage whatever offended dignity my board is currently pretending they feel? Tell me what it is you need, I shall provide it, and then we can all move on with our lives."

That felt like a slap, and the fact that it did made her wonder why she hadn't noticed that he was getting to her the way he was. Not just that *thing* she could still feel like a new pulse, low in her belly. He was nice to look at, yes—magnetic, even—but it was more than that. She was leaning forward in the uncomfortable chair she'd chosen and now felt she had to pretend she found pleasant.

But Sarina wasn't assessing Matteo Combe the way she should have been. Instead, she was hanging on his every word. She was enjoying sparring with him a little bit too much.

She was…*enjoying* this. *Him.*

A wave of self-hatred crashed over her, and on some level she was shocked it didn't sweep her away. That he couldn't see it.

I'm sorry, Jeanette. And as she thought of her lost friend, her sister in her soul, another wave hit her—this time, of the grief that never quite left her. And never would, she thought, until she did her part to give a little back to the kind of men who preyed on pretty girls like Jeanette had been. And did nothing when they fell apart, because they'd already moved on to another victim.

Sarina had vowed that she would honor her best friend's memory right there where she'd found Jeanette's body, there in the bathroom of the apartment they'd shared while Sarina finished up her graduate work. She would do what she could to bring supposedly untouchable men to justice, if they deserved it. She would identify predators, look hard at arrogance, and where appropriate, help dismantle systems that kept abusive men in power.

That vow hadn't simply been words. She'd made it the cornerstone of her life.

One beautiful, brooding much-too-rich man with eyes like smoke wasn't going to change that.

"I'm afraid that's not how it works." Her voice was much chillier than it had been before. Overcompensation, maybe. But there was something about Matteo that encouraged her to…lean in too much. Be a little bit too much engaged. Try to match wits with him when she should have been quietly and competently undermining his confidence. "I understand that you're a man who's used to being in charge of things, but you're not in charge of this. I am. I will tell you when and where the next meeting is. You already agreed to show up. In the same fashion, I will let you know when we're finished."

"Surely you cannot have convinced my board to allow this to drag on forever. They prefer instant gratification, I must tell you."

"What I did or did not offer your board isn't something I can discuss with you. They are my client. The nature of our relationship must remain private."

"How convenient."

"Here's what I want you to think about," she said, and smiled at him, encouragingly. With too much teeth, perhaps. "Control is obviously very important to you. You control your company, now more than ever. You apparently think that you ought to be able to control the reproductive choices of your own sister. You're a very powerful man, and powerful men, as a rule, tend to be under the impression that they should be able to control anything and everything. But you don't control this. You don't control me."

"As it happens, I have thought of little else."

Again, he was far more dry than she'd been prepared for. It unnerved her—but Sarina hid that. Or hoped she did.

"Good. And as you continue to think about it, as I'm sure you will, I'd like you to find your way to viewing this as an opportunity."

His mouth curved into something sardonic. "An opportunity for what, exactly?"

He was still leaning forward, and despite herself, so was she. And the room suddenly felt breathless. Fraught and tight around them, like a fist.

But Sarina didn't sit back. She didn't break that connection—because she refused to show him that she noticed it in the first place.

"Why, for you, Mr. Combe." She made her voice light. Very nearly airy. "It's your opportunity to be a better person. Once you learn how to give up control, you might find that you don't have to struggle with concepts like toxic masculinity."

His expression suggested that he was not over-concerned with said concepts, or indeed any kind of struggle. But he only gazed back at her, his gray eyes steady in a way that made her breath feel shallow.

"And I will be free of this struggle because my corporation will crumble into dust, as it requires my control and attention at all times? Or perhaps it will be my family that suffers, once I release my grip—as I am the only thing currently holding us together? I think you misunderstand the fundamental nature of my character, Dr. Fellows. I am not trying to control the universe. Between you and me, I do not much care about the universe. But I do like to control what I am, in fact, in control of."

"Says the man who descended into an all-out brawl at his own father's funeral."

She saw it then. That blaze of pure, stark temper in his gaze that made his whole face change. Into something taut and dark. Powerful in an entirely different way.

Thrilling, something in her supplied, as she pulsed anew. But she ignored all of that.

Or she tried.

But Matteo's eyes were smoke and ruin, and she had the oddest sense he knew it.

"Oh, Doctor." He sounded almost pitying. Almost. "Do you think that I was goaded into punching that man? On the contrary, I very much meant to do that. And am glad I did."

CHAPTER THREE

MATTEO SHOULD NOT have said that.

It was the truth, but the truth was needlessly provocative and he'd known it even as he'd formed the words.

Sarina had stood, a curious expression on her face. *Triumphant,* he'd thought in the moment, though he couldn't think why. She'd smoothed her hands over her skirt as if to free it from wrinkles, though it showed none, and when she'd gazed at him her expression had been nothing short of pitying.

"I think we'll stop here," she had said in that way of hers, as if her word was law in Matteo's house. In his presence. When everyone else who'd ever dared speak to him like that had been related to him by blood—and was now dead. "Before we stray too far from our objectives. And I'd advise you to take a bit of time to reflect on the opportunity you have before you for growth, Mr. Combe.

But that growth will be stagnant, I fear, if you remain completely unrepentant for the unprovoked physical attack you made on another man."

At least that time he'd had the sense to bite his tongue.

And he'd reflected, all right, but not in the way the doctor had ordered. She had refused his offer of accommodation, which was likely wise when he couldn't seem to keep himself from looking at her in ways he knew he shouldn't. She'd let herself out of the library and marched off, down from his preferred wing of the villa into the great hall, where she'd stood, prim and disapproving, in the midst of all his San Giacomo ancestors in their fussy portraits.

He'd reflected on the height of her heels, sharp stilettos that made her legs look longer than they were and gave rise to all manner of inappropriate images in his head. One more delicious than the next. He'd reflected on the cool intelligence in her gaze and how much he liked that, even when she clearly wished to use it against him. Maybe especially then, because he couldn't seem to help but like a challenge. He'd reflected that, really, it was unfortunate that he found his board-appointed therapist—*consultant*—so mouthwatering. Intellectually as well as physically.

He spared no thought at all to Prince Ares,

whose eye he'd happily blackened. And would again, with a song in his heart.

Matteo had waited quietly with Sarina until the boat was brought around to ferry her back to her hotel, and he'd murmured all the appropriate, polite things as she'd gone back out into the rain.

But he knew his first meeting with this woman had not gone as well as it might have.

And if he hadn't, a board member who was still his ally rang up the following morning to quote Matteo's words back to him.

"You meant to punch that prince. You said so straight out." Lord Christopher Radcliffe sounded despairing. "Do you *want* them to vote you out of power, Matteo? Is that what this is about? Suicide by board meeting?"

"Of course not," Matteo had replied,

But that wasn't entirely true. There was a part of him that wanted nothing more than to light it all on fire and walk away.

Sometimes that part of him made a lot of noise.

It was shouting up a storm as he flew back to London two days later.

By then he'd had every member of his board on the phone to him, demanding he explain the report they'd received from the consultant Matteo had known was in their pocket—but perhaps not so deep. He'd learned a valuable lesson.

His instincts about Sarina Fellows had been correct: she wanted to take him down.

He was pleased to have that clarified, he thought darkly as his plane soared over continental Europe. He should have thought of that while he was letting her provoke him into shooting off his mouth. He should have been prepared for the woman to be a weapon, and he hadn't been—because he'd been far more intrigued by the gut punch of his attraction to her.

And as entertaining as it was to imagine the fun he might have had with a woman like Sarina if he'd met her under different circumstances, Matteo couldn't actually let her take him down. He had felt compelled to allow his board to subject him to this consultation, and thought submitting to it as his own father wouldn't have made him look far more reasonable and biddable than Eddie had been, but he couldn't let her plant her seeds of doubt and dissension. It would never be a good time for such things, but this was particularly bad timing all around. He needed to prove to a set of disapproving old men that he could take the helm of the company he'd already been running for years. He needed to cater to his family's legacy and make sure Combe Industries didn't die on his watch. And while he was at it, he needed to handle all the unpleasant revelations of his parents' wills.

No matter how much the consultant his board had selected got to him.

He might have the odd daydream of walking away from it all, but he never would. That wasn't who he was.

Matteo was the eldest son—or he'd spent his life thinking he was, anyway—and he had been raised to clean up any and all messes that arose on both sides of his family. He was the heir to the San Giacomo legacy. He was president and CEO of Combe Industries. And more than that, he was the family janitor.

What Matteo did was clean up the mess, whatever it was.

Whether he wanted to or not.

At least this particular mess was of his own making. He was the one who had taken that swing at Prince Ares—and to the other man's credit, little as Matteo wanted to give him any when he'd already helped himself to Pia, he'd taken the hit. And had then done the right thing by Pia by instantly proposing marriage. It was the paparazzi who'd carried on as if Matteo had sucker punched him and left him for dead.

Everything else on Matteo's plate was there courtesy of someone else's inability to handle their lives the way he did. His sister's love life and its consequences no matter his or anyone's feelings on the matter, like the princely proposal she'd had no choice but to accept—as she was carrying the heir to the throne of the island kingdom of Atilia. Or his parents' indiscretions and old scandals made new now that they'd died, in the form of at least one sibling Matteo hadn't known he had—and wasn't sure how to deal with now he did.

It was one hit after the next, and really, what was a slanted psychological evaluation complete with a not-so-hidden agenda next to family members he'd never met?

To say nothing about the company that he still had to run whether his board of directors thought he was fit for it or not.

By the time he landed in London, Matteo had been putting out fires for hours. Those of his own making and all the others that cropped up every day of the week. And he had little to look forward to but another long day—and week, and month— with more of the same. Fires everywhere, and once again, it was his job to extinguish them. And despite what his board pretended to think, or the papers brayed daily, the one thing Matteo had always been very, very good at was his job.

The thing about putting out fires for the whole of a man's adult life was that, sooner or later, he developed a taste for the flames. An appreciation and something akin to admiration.

His father had set out to crush those flames any

way he could. Matteo preferred to exult in them, then use the resulting heat to his advantage.

And that was what he chose to reflect upon, just as the doctor had ordered. It appeared Sarina wanted to play games instead of plod through the expected set of sessions in good faith. Matteo was perfectly happy to play along now that he'd sussed out her intentions—because the truth was, when it came to games of high stakes where winning meant surviving, he always won.

"I'm sorry to interrupt," his personal assistant, Lauren, said one morning a few days after that first session in Venice, standing at his desk in London in her usual no-nonsense manner, which was one of the reasons he paid her so well. "But she's here, I'm afraid. And insists upon seeing you."

Matteo was neck deep in contract negotiations with foreign distributors—all of whom had spent the past month reading the tabloids, apparently—and couldn't think of a single person with a claim to his time. Or anyone who would dare send his assistant in here to demand it.

He scowled. "And who is *she,* may I ask? The bloody Queen?"

Lauren Clarke had been working for him for far too long to react to that tone of his. Or the ferocious glare he leveled at her.

"Not the Queen, sir. I doubt very much she'd appear without an appointment and the royal guard. It's that psychiatrist."

And this was part of what he'd agreed to, purely to placate the board. They'd all been foaming at the mouth, waving tabloid magazines and their fists in the air, and caterwauling as if they'd expected the building to fall down around their ears. He'd have agreed to anything to calm them down, and he had.

So now he had a psychiatrist standing in his office, demanding to be seen. In the middle of a complicated workday—which was to say, any old Tuesday at Combe Industries.

But he was no longer operating in good faith. She wanted to play with matches? Matteo would respond with a bonfire.

Something inside him rolled over, shook itself off, and bared its teeth.

He finished his call and gazed back at his PA, though he didn't see her. He saw Sarina instead, and that sheen of triumph all over her face in Venice.

"Give me five minutes," he instructed Lauren. "Then show her in."

He set his trap, then moved to the windows that looked out over the city. Night had already set in, gloomy and wet though it was supposedly spring out there. He could see the suggestion of light and movement, blurred with moisture.

But however cold and miserable it was outside,

it was no match for the blast of heat he felt when he heard his office door open, then shut.

Temper. Fury. Anticipation.

"You have been busy, Doctor," he said, his voice so mild he almost fooled himself into imagining it was real. "In less than a week you have managed to sow dissent throughout the whole of Combe Industries. Uncertainty and speculation."

"I don't know what you mean, Mr. Combe," came the reply in her smooth voice, and maybe he was imagining the undercurrent of satisfaction in it. Though he doubted it. "I told you that you weren't my client. You should have assumed that anything you said to me was in no way confidential."

Matteo didn't turn around to face her. He kept his gaze on the window before him, but he stopped looking at blurry, giddy London, and focused instead on the figure he could see in the reflection.

She was dressed in black again, sleek and sharp. *Like a blade*, he thought.

And he was certain he could feel every hair on his body stand on end. He told himself it was his temper channeling into the ferocious intent he was known for, nothing more. This woman had no idea what he was capable of—but he had every intention of showing her.

"I did not expect confidentiality," Matteo replied. "But I did imagine you would pretend, at the very least, to get at the truth. Instead, you have made it clear that your mission is to destroy me."

He waited for her to deny that, but she didn't.

She didn't laugh, either, but he was sure he could hear the hint of it in her voice when she answered him. "I don't need to destroy you. You appear to being doing that job all by yourself."

"I was under the impression that you were here to perform an impartial assessment, not an assassination."

She moved farther into his vast, sprawling office. He watched her reflection move across the room, a liquid, rolling walk, all hips and glory, and he stopped pretending that the way she affected him had only to do with his temper. She was wearing another pair of those impossible heels, and Matteo was forced to face the somewhat confronting notion that this woman was not only doing her best to make a fool out of him in front of his business associates—she was single-handedly turning him into a foot fetishist.

He would make her pay for that, too.

"I'm not following you," came her cool reply. He watched her walk to the front of his desk, then shift to lean against it. She folded her arms over her chest, she cocked out one hip, and he knew she understood every square inch of the power games she was playing. At another time he might have applauded it. "I assume you feel that your character is being assassinated, is that it?"

"With a hatchet, Dr. Fellows."

He didn't have to see that smirk of hers to feel it, like one more knife shoved deep into his back. "Your character is your business, Mr. Combe. You explained to me that you felt justified in all of your choices. How, then, could I take a hatchet to your good name? Surely that would only be possible if you felt some sense of shame."

"Because you are determined, one way or another, that you will make me feel this shame. No matter what it takes."

"That you're even discussing the possibility of feeling shame feels a great deal like a breakthrough. I didn't think such a thing was possible."

He turned then, holding on to his control by the barest of threads. He could feel temper, yes, but something far darker—and much thicker—pounding in his veins. Making his skin feel too tight. Making his self-possession feel threadbare at best.

But then, this was where he had always operated at his fullest capacity. When he was the most challenged, he shone the brightest.

He hoped he blinded her.

"You will have to tell me what you think it will take," he growled at her. "Do you require me on my knees? Shall I rend my garments at your whim? You will obviously only be satisfied by a very specific performance. Why don't you tell me my lines?"

Her smile was placid, but her dark eyes gleamed. "If it is not genuine, Mr. Combe, how can it be counted as real?"

"Tell me, Doctor. How would you know the first thing about genuine sentiment for one's family?"

He took satisfaction in the way she stiffened, as if she hadn't expected the hit. Her gaze flashed into something darker and he liked that, too.

"I would strongly caution you against making this personal," she said, and this time her voice was stern. As if she thought he might back down simply because she sounded like she was in charge.

But Matteo wasn't her client. As she had amply illustrated.

"Why ever not, Dr. Fellows?" he asked, his voice quiet. But he could tell by the way her chin lifted that she wasn't fooled by his tone. "My board of directors feels that they can excavate my personal life at will. Why shouldn't I do the same with the blunt instrument they have sent to do their bidding?"

"Am I...a *tool* in this scenario?"

"What you are is a woman who has no experience whatsoever in the sorts of relationships that led me to the choices I made at my father's funeral."

"You don't think I'm capable of assessing human relationships. Is that what you just said?"

Matteo felt everything in him focus on his target, and thrust his hands into the pockets of his suit trousers before he reached out with them and ruined this little trail of breadcrumbs he was leaving for her.

"Your parents are lofty intellectuals," he told her, as if she might have missed that. "Academics who have spent their lives locked away in elite institutions, catering to children of the rich and famous."

"I'm going to stand back and wait for the irony to hit. If I were you, I would duck."

"They had you when they were quite old, relatively speaking. You have no siblings. As your parents were each only children themselves, you have no extended family of any kind. Which made it doubly challenging, I imagine, that they ignored you so thoroughly as you grew up, if their lack of attendance at what might reasonably be considered your milestones is any guide. What I'm suggesting to you is that when it comes to the kinds of familial bonds and debts that govern the lives of most people, your view is necessarily limited by your experience."

"I live in the world," she shot back at him, with heat, and he wondered if she knew that she'd betrayed herself. That he could see he'd landed a hit.

"Last I checked, the world was filled with human beings and human relationships. In fact, I made those things the focus of my life's work. Rest assured that even if I never experienced the delight of a house filled with siblings—or even numerous houses shared with one much younger sibling and a whole lot of staff, like you—I have made a deep and comprehensive study of every possible permutation of human emotion."

"Furthermore," he said, the way he would if he was in a business meeting and didn't wish to acknowledge that someone else had spoken, "you appear to lack any actual personal relationships yourself."

She flushed at that, which told him a great many things he doubted very much she wanted him to know. Then she stood straighter, and he was sure he could see her vibrating with her own temper.

But unless he missed his guess, with decidedly less focus.

"You have absolutely no right to go digging around in my life," she hurled at him.

"It seems only fair. Since you've taken a backhoe to mine."

"You do realize, of course, that this is more evidence of the kind of antisocial behavior that got you into this position in the first place?"

"I am a man who does my research. I leave nothing to chance. No one who knows me—particularly my board—could possibly imagine that I would allow someone access to me, my thoughts, my entire life, and not perform my due diligence."

"You must be very proud of yourself," Sarina said, after a moment, that flush still betraying her emotions. He wanted to touch the heat of it. Taste it, even. "Does it make you feel more in control of this downward spiral of yours to think you've unearthed the truth about me?"

"You have no relationships," he repeated, as if he was delivering judgment from above. "You're a driven, ambitious, professional woman. You live and breathe your work, and you usually do both from hotels. Your parents are fully preoccupied with their research. As far as I can tell, you are entirely solitary."

They were standing, facing off, as if a brawl was about to break out. And Matteo knew that he was his father's son, because his blood sang at the thought. But he was also heir to the San Giacomos and all the scheming and plotting that had made them one of Italy's most prominent families—for centuries.

Sarina should have done her homework.

"You must be under the impression that if you taunt me with my own life, this will somehow… Break me? Put me off my game? Unfortunately for you, Mr. Combe, all it does is give me further insight into your character. I wouldn't be concerned about anyone else performing an assassination when you seem so willing and able to do it yourself."

She'd wrestled that flush on her cheeks into submission. Now she gazed back at him pityingly, which he assumed was meant to make him feel small. Off balance.

But Matteo could see the way her pulse racketed around in her neck, and he knew better.

That response—the response he'd thought he'd seen in Venice, but hadn't pushed—was what he'd been banking on. Somehow, he contained his own roar of victory.

"It turns out I have a fascination for psychology," he said instead. "For example, I cannot help but wonder why a woman who lives such a lonely, empty life imagines that she should set herself up as a world-renowned expert on the very emotions and relationships she lacks? I should as soon declare myself an authority on literature. I've read a book, after all."

"Keep digging that hole, Mr. Combe."

Matteo moved then, prowling closer to her and keeping his eyes on that telltale pulse. It was possible it was her own temper, of course. But when he moved closer, he saw the way her eyes widened. The slight flare of her nostrils. And, sure enough, that pulse in her neck sped up.

He knew attraction when he saw it. He felt an answering lick of fire in his own body.

And that triumph beneath it like a naked flame.

"This is very personal for you, is it not?" He stopped when he was within arm's reach, close enough that he could see the faint tremor that ran over her skin "There is nothing the least bit clinical about this meeting. Or the previous one. You are here to perform a hit job, no more and no less."

She shook her head, but he knew she could feel the heat between them—growing stronger by the second the longer they stayed in such close proximity—because he could.

Sarina cleared her throat. "You must realize that every single word that comes out of your mouth is a nail that you, and you alone, are hammering into your own coffin."

But then she lifted her hand. He thought perhaps she meant to mime the hammering of a nail. Or perhaps she meant to swat at him. He would never know.

Because what she did instead was…place it on his chest. In the hollow between his pectoral muscles.

And for a simmering moment, they both stared at her hand.

While everything went electric.

When Matteo lifted his gaze to hers, he saw more heat on her cheeks—and a kind of horrified confusion all over her face. While around them, the world simmered and burned.

She started to snatch her hand back but he caught it and held it there. Then pressed his advantage, leaning closer, straight into all that fire.

"I understand that you are nothing but a mouthpiece," he said, low and dark, like love words in the middle of a very long night. She shivered. "A recording device that plays back my every utterance so that my enemies can cluck and shake their heads and pretend to be affronted."

Her hand flexed against his chest. It made a mockery of her attempt at an icy expression and he thought she knew it, because there was still too much heat. Lightning and thunder, and he wasn't prepared for any of it.

But that didn't mean he wouldn't use it.

"Or, alternatively, I report back to my client," she said, though her color was still too high. "Which is perfectly appropriate."

Matteo let her go, noting exactly how long it took her to notice he'd released her. And then to pull her hand back. As if she'd accidentally slapped it down on a hot stovetop and had only then realized it.

He waited a moment, but the heat storm kept raging, loud and hot. He slid his palm down over her jaw, holding his hand there.

Holding her right where he wanted her.

The heat was extraordinary. It raged in him, thick and insistent. And he could feel the way she trembled at his touch, and that kicked in him hard. So hard he almost forgot what game he was playing.

"What exactly do you think you're doing?" she asked, though her voice was different now. Almost breathy. Soft and uncertain, like that odd, arrested look in her eyes. And the fact she didn't pull away.

But he wasn't here to understand her. He was here to win.

No matter that her skin felt like silk, warmed through and made specifically for him.

"Were you attempting to show me that you were in control when you put your hand on me?" he asked quietly. "Without asking? I think in some quarters, that's considered the very definition of toxic behavior, is it not?"

"It was a moment of temporary insanity," Sarina replied, but without so much as a trace of her usual smirk.

And the battle was won. Matteo knew it.

But her cheek in his hand was soft, warm. And he could feel the jolt of it, straight down into his sex, like a promise. Those precarious heels she wore with such ease put her mouth right there within reach, and all he'd have to do was bend his head to lose himself in her taste. Her heat.

The sweetness he was sure was there, right under the surface—

"Mr. Combe."

Her voice was crisper then. Very nearly the matter-of-fact tone he recalled from Venice. He was certain she was going to order him away from her—

But she didn't. She didn't jerk her head out of his grasp. She didn't tell him to step back. She didn't flinch, or shout, or threaten him. She gazed back at him as if this was all out of her hands.

Or as if she didn't know what was roaring there between them any more than he did.

He could feel that pulse of hers, telling him truths he was certain she never would.

And echoing his own, the one that whispered he was risking his own destruction here.

"If we're nailing my coffin shut," Matteo murmured, because she felt like silk, he wanted to rub his way all over her, and he should have been afraid of the ferocity of his reaction and the fire that raged between them—yet he still wanted to win, "we had best make certain it is airtight."

And then he bent his head and tasted that clever mouth of hers.

At last.

CHAPTER FOUR

SARINA WAS BETRAYING herself in every possible way and she didn't know why.

Or how.

Only that she couldn't seem to stop.

She had walked into this office in full control. Of herself—and of Matteo, she'd been certain. She had delivered her first report to her clients when she'd returned to her hotel that night in Venice and had been gratified not only with how thankful they were, but how eager they'd seemed to hear each and every opinion she had on the topic of their deeply problematic CEO.

Dropping by unexpectedly on her various subjects was one of her favorite tricks. Backed into a corner, powerful men either rose to the occasion or, like Matteo, responded badly.

She'd had death threats. Red faces and bulging veins, with promises to rip her limb from limb. She'd been propositioned, bribed, and once—

memorably—had been forcibly removed from the premises by a security team.

Sarina had delighted in each and every over-the-top, rage-soaked response. Each time a man responded that way, it confirmed she was absolutely right to do the work she did. To divide the good from the corrupt, then take the bad ones down, one by one, so they couldn't use their wealth and power to hurt others.

And if there was the odd bit of discomfort in that, or even just the fear of it, she was always more than happy to put herself on the line. She knew in her heart that Jeanette would have done the same for her had their situations been reversed. Jeanette, who had been the one to teach Sarina how to stand up for herself in the first place. Jeanette, who had been the scourge of the would-be bullies in their elementary school. Jeannette, who had taught Sarina that there was almost nothing that couldn't be solved with a belly laugh and the liberal application of ice cream.

But this was something else entirely.

Matteo was completely outside of her experience—and he was kissing her like he knew every single sinful thing her body was capable of when Sarina wasn't sure she did.

She should never have touched him. She didn't know why she had. Why her hand had taken on a life of its own and found its way to his chest—and then stayed there. And she should have slapped him the moment he'd put his hand on her face, but she hadn't, and she didn't know why.

Liar, a little voice inside her whispered then. *You know exactly why.*

And it was this.

It was his mouth on hers, hot and demanding.

It was his taste, male and heady and astonishingly addictive.

He was ruin and temptation and as if he knew it, he angled his head and took the kiss deeper. Wilder.

And all of that was bad enough.

But then Sarina forgot herself entirely, forgot everything she had ever vowed or believed, and kissed him back.

And everything…slid out of place.

It shifted, igniting inside of her. Then it exploded.

There was no other way to explain how her arms ended up wrapped around his neck. How he didn't move a muscle and yet she surged up on her toes, plastering herself against the front of that dark, absurdly well-fitting suit that did nothing to erase her memories of his biceps and that T-shirt back in Venice.

None of it made sense, but he tasted like fire and he taught her about need.

One luxuriant slide of his tongue against hers at a time.

Sarina felt intoxicated. Drunk inside and out, while her breasts ached for more, and between her legs, what had been a pulse in that villa in Venice became something more like a drumbeat.

He was the one who pulled his mouth away, and Sarina let out a small, greedy sort of sound she would have assured anyone who asked she wasn't capable of making.

Matteo's dark eyes glittered, smoke and need.

"Make certain you give every detail of that kiss when you deliver your report," he rasped at her, his voice like gravel, though she could feel it all over her—inside and out—like a terrible caress. "I would not wish the board to miss a single detail of your response, enthusiastic as it was."

Shame slammed into her, thick and dark. Sarina pushed back away from him the way she should have done from the start, but it was useless. She could put space between them, she could marinate in her own dawning horror at what she'd just done—*enthusiastically,* as he'd said—but there was no pretending it hadn't happened.

There was no lying to herself about who and what she'd betrayed here.

When what she'd come to do was gloat. Take the knife and drive it in deeper.

What had *happened* to her?

"No razor-sharp comeback?" Matteo taunted her, no trace of shame on his beautiful face. "No pointed questions like a scalpel, the better to dice me into bite-size pieces? I'm disappointed in you, Doctor."

Sarina tried to pull herself together. Her mind reeled from one half-formed, desperate thought to the next.

"I don't think you understand how badly it will look for you when I tell your board that you decided to put your hands on me," she pointed out.

And she didn't understand what she saw flash over his face then. It looked too much like victory.

Then his mouth curved, making it worse. Making everything worse. "Tell them. Explain to them, in detail, what a brute I am. I welcome it."

Sarina had never considered herself a liar. But that empty feeling in her stomach when she imagined saying so out loud, to a man like Matteo, made her realize that it was unlikely anyone in his position would believe that of her. It was unlikely any of the men she'd identified as deserving targets thought she was honest, and least of all him.

He fully expected her to claim he was a brute, even though both he and she knew better.

For the first time since she'd started down this road, she felt her sense of purpose…shake a bit, down into its foundations.

But she pushed on. "It will be my word against

yours without resorting to calling anyone a brute, Mr. Combe."

"Matteo," he corrected her, his voice dark and sinful. "You had your tongue in my mouth. You had best use my Christian name, don't you think?"

That thudded through her like some kind of gong. A warning, though she was terribly afraid it was already too late.

Sarina tried to remember herself. To stand straight and get back on track, the way she always did. "It will be my word against yours no matter what I call you. And I suspect you know as well as I do that your board is far more likely to find my word convincing than yours."

She expected him to bluster then. To scowl ferociously at her, then vent his spleen, the way men like him always did.

But Matteo Combe only smiled.

And Sarina could feel it like a flash flood, everywhere, drowning her where she stood. Closing over her head and sucking her down.

She wasn't sure she could breathe, or if she should try, and that wasn't even addressing the glittering look in those smoke-colored eyes.

"I wouldn't be so sure about that," he said, and there was something more than triumph in his voice then. Something that felt to her like a shudder beneath her own skin. "You may find that while my board is more than happy to convict me in absentia to line their own pockets, when it comes down to it, they are a group of extraordinarily conservative men. Deeply traditional and possessed, I regret to tell you, of all the regressive notions you would expect of men like them."

She told herself there was no reason her heart should be kicking at her like that, as if she was in some kind of panic when she wasn't. Of course she wasn't.

Sarina was the only one who knew how she'd betrayed herself here. How, in the space of one kiss, she'd broken every promise she'd ever made to the girl she still considered her sister.

One terrible, life-altering kiss she still couldn't process. Her lips felt…raw, almost. Or maybe she did. Everywhere.

"You aren't making any sense," she managed to say, though her heart was still thumping in her chest. "The board of directors of any major corporation is generally conservative, yes. That's not news."

And it was why she'd always made certain to conduct herself in a manner above reproach. Until today.

"Indeed." Matteo slid his hands into the pockets of his trousers again, and she couldn't help noticing that he looked entirely too satisfied with himself. A trickle of something she refused to call fear made its way down her spine. "How do you imagine such a conservative group would react to a video of you plastering yourself against me? Between you and me, Sarina, I like my chances."

She went hot, then cold. Then even hotter than before. An intense emotion she couldn't name flashed through her, threatening to come out in furious tears—the very thought of which horrified her.

"Don't be ridiculous. You only wish you had a video." She didn't even know where those words came from. But she sounded tough and unbothered, neither of which she felt in any way, shape, or form, so she decided to roll with it.

"I regret to inform you that I am a man of action, not wishes."

Matteo belted out a verbal command, seemingly to the air, then lifted his chin in the direction of the far wall.

Where, to Sarina's horror, the wood paneling pulled back and a screen appeared.

And for a dizzying moment, she thought it was entirely possible she might be sick. Or pass out. Or both.

"You must know that it is, at the very least, unethical to record—"

Matteo laughed. "Do you really think this is the time for a discussion of ethics?"

Sarina stared at the blank screen before her. Her throat was dry, yet those tears still threatened.

"I don't believe you," she said, trying to sound bold as she called his bluff.

"It never occurred to me that you would," he replied. Much too smoothly.

He called out another command, and the video began to play.

And Sarina had been here. Right here in this room, a party to everything she was watching unfold before her on that damned screen. She had been here, she knew she'd participated, and yet she still couldn't make sense of what she saw before her.

In her head she had stridden in so confidently, secure in the knowledge that she had yet another captain of industry in the palm of her hand, which was precisely where she liked them.

But the woman she saw on-screen abandoned her position of power almost immediately. She moved too close to Matteo, for one thing. And while Sarina remembered what she'd said, and how cool and professional she tried to sound, her body told a different story.

A significantly more flirtatious one, to her horror.

Even before they reached the part where she had so foolishly reached out and put her hand on him, she was horrified.

And then he kissed her, and that was worse.

For one thing, watching herself kiss him was

like doing it all over again. All that heat and the dark mastery of his mouth on hers shot through her, making her shake where she stood.

But more appalling still, the woman on screen… melted.

There was no other word to describe it. *She* was the one who'd moved closer. *She* was the one who wrapped herself around him.

She was a looking at a stranger, but the stranger was herself.

"Oh dear," Matteo murmured, his voice bright with feigned concern. "This does not look good for our fearless doctor."

Sarina scraped herself together, somehow, though she could hardly tell what was part of her and what wasn't. She felt wrecked in ways she could hardly count, but she would deal with that later. She would repair to her hotel room, take a long, hard look in the mirror, and figure out where on earth that woman on-screen had come from. She would figure out how she had let this happen in the first place and what it meant that she had so misread one of her targets.

But she would do all that in private.

First she had to extricate herself from the mess she'd made here.

"Congratulations, Mr. Combe," she managed to say, her voice so icy she was surprised a glacier didn't fall out of her mouth. She turned to face him, and held herself as still as she could get. Her spine was so straight she was dimly amazed it didn't snap in half. "You have outmaneuvered me. I'm woman enough to admit it. Congratulations. But I should warn you, the chairman of your board seems highly motivated to continue with this assessment. You can fire me, but it's a certainty that he will have me replaced."

"You misunderstand me entirely, Sarina," Matteo said, a rich current of something deep and male running through his voice that she didn't want to hear, much less name. "You're not going anywhere. The game has changed, that's all. But I'm going to require you to keep playing it."

She'd wrapped herself in ice in an attempt to get her feet back under her, but she felt it turn to slush at that. "I don't know what you mean."

"I could show that tape to my board, or I could show it to the world." He shrugged, and she didn't mistake the look in his dark eyes then. He relished this. And on some level, she wasn't sure she blamed him—which told her more things about herself she didn't want to know. "Your choice."

"I want to be absolutely certain I understand you," she said, clearing her throat as she desperately tried to find some leverage. "You are standing here in front of me, threatening to slut shame me on the global stage with a video recording that you must know is illegal."

"I invite and encourage you to find a single member of the paparazzi who will give a toss about the legal ramifications of that video, Sarina. Please. Knock yourself out."

"No one gives a toss about anything until they find themselves sued for it, I imagine."

"But the damage will already be done, will it not?" His smile was razor sharp, and it dawned on her belatedly that she had completely underestimated him. She'd imagined he was like all the rest, when he wasn't. He was worse. "Your reputation depends on your ability to move through the corporate world like a shark, taking down your prey swiftly and with prejudice. But how will you do that when everybody knows you might also fling yourself at your quarry in a romantic fervor?"

There was no leverage here, but Sarina kept trying to find a way out.

"Let me guess, you're going to pretend that you're not blackmailing me…but you'll require demeaning and disgusting sexual favors to make certain of it."

"So you can martyr yourself on the altar of my lust, content to think me the monster you imagined me when you walked into my villa in Venice? I think not."

"Of course you're not a *monster*. Silly me. Recording someone without their knowledge is perfectly normal, not monstrous at all."

Matteo laughed at her acid tone. "And this is absolutely blackmail. No need to mince words, is there? But I don't require sexual favors from you, Sarina. Not as payments, anyway. What you choose to bestow is entirely up to you." His dark gaze…did things to her. She could feel her breasts ache again, as if she was still pressing herself against him. As if her body was attuned to him in ways that made no sense at all. "And my preference would not be for demeaning or disgusting acts, but I pride myself on being open-minded when it comes to matters of the flesh. Feel free to convince me otherwise."

"And if I choose not to bestow any acts upon you at all?"

"As you wish." His expression didn't change. There was no reason at all Sarina should have felt a hollow place yawn open inside of her, as if she'd lost something. "But as it happens, I am less interested in what you can do for me in bed. It's what you can do for me in the boardroom that interests me."

Sarina assured herself that that rocking, shipwrecked sensation was relief. Because she didn't think she had it in her to perform a sexual favor on command, no matter what she had to lose if she didn't. And yet she knew that he was absolutely right about the damage that video would do to her career if he released it. And she was—or she should have been—giddy with relief that she wouldn't have to test what kind of person she really was.

She told herself she couldn't feel the molten heat between her legs that suggested to her that her true feelings on the subject were far more complicated.

"You want me to lie to your board."

"Not at all," Matteo replied, sounding very nearly entertained. She hated him. "I want you to give them the glowing account of my fitness for my duties that I deserve. No more and no less."

And Sarina wanted to gather her cloak of righteousness around her. She wanted to draw herself up to a great height and cut this man down with the force of her integrity. Because she had started this for the best of reasons, hadn't she? She had watched what that man had done to Jeanette, how he'd destroyed her, and she had vowed that she would see to it that he couldn't do it to anyone else. He had been the first corporate giant she had helped remove from his position, and she still held that victory close to her heart. Nothing could bring Jeanette back, but Sarina had been so sure that what she'd done to the man who'd abused her had restored a little balance.

But Sarina hadn't stopped there. She'd spent the years in between going out of her way to make herself available to anyone and everyone who needed her services—and she'd told herself that there was nothing wrong with that. That it wasn't her fault there were so many men like this in the world, wholly deserving of the kinds of consequences that she alone could deliver. There were good, decent men, too, of course. But the scales seemed to tip toward the unpleasant ones.

And somewhere in there she had lost track of herself, and maybe those scales, too…or she wouldn't be here today.

Somewhere in there, she had become the vigilante she'd told Matteo he was. The cowboy who swaggered into town and shot the place up because she could, because she was good with a gun, and because she enjoyed a firefight—not because she was needed.

Because she had seen the pictures from Eddie Combe's funeral splashed across the tabloids. Yes, Matteo had punched broodingly handsome Prince Ares in the face. But Matteo's sister hadn't looked the least bit horrified by the display. And if Sarina was being completely honest with herself, neither had the prince.

Why do you imagine that what you think about a situation matters more than what those involved in it feel? a voice inside her asked.

Because she had long since stopped caring whether the outrage she operated in was manufactured or not. She'd long ago stopped caring either way. If there was outrage, she acted.

Is this really who you are? that voice asked.

A voice she recognized. A voice that sounded like the best friend and sister she'd lost so long ago.

At a certain point—or maybe at this particular point, whether she wanted to or not—Sarina wondered whether she wasn't punishing abuses of power anymore. If instead, she was committing them herself when called in by questionable people like the chairman of the Combe Industries board, who had told her straight off he wanted Matteo gone.

She didn't want to answer those questions inside her. Though she was afraid the fact she'd asked them already gave her the answers.

Sarina felt shaken straight through when she returned her attention to the man standing there in front of her, watching and waiting as if he could see every thought that moved through her. As if he already knew how this would end.

"I don't want that video released anywhere," she said when she was sure she could speak without stammering or shaking. When she could sound like a version of her former self. "Why don't you tell me what it is you want me to do."

She told herself that this would be a spot of penance, that was all, which never hurt anyone. And it could be worse, of course. If Matteo still required that she deliver her findings to his board, that suggested that he wouldn't press his advantage as far as others might have. Surely that gave her some kind of armor. She could pay her penance and even learn a little something from this experience. Like how not to repeat it. And while she was at it, maybe she could go on and change her life back to something— and herself to someone—she recognized.

Assuming she survived this.

Something that seemed significantly in doubt when all Matteo Combe did was smile back at her, like a wolf.

CHAPTER FIVE

THE COMBE FAMILY seat sprawled across the better part of the highest hill outside one of Yorkshire's old industrial mill towns. Many of the original mill structures had been reclaimed these days, turned into gastropubs, highly optimistic boutiques, and modernized flats, in a concerted effort to draw a younger, flasher demographic back to these once-abandoned northern towns.

But Combe Manor had been built a long time ago for a very different purpose: to proclaim the Combe family's precipitous rise from their humble beginnings to all and sundry. Its purpose was to be seen from all corners of the village.

Which meant it stood apart from that village, up a winding road with no neighbors within shouting distance. Isolated and out of reach in every possible way, Sarina couldn't help but notice.

But she assumed that was the point.

And her pounding heart, newly in residence in

the back of her throat, would simply have to find a way to cope.

Matteo had insisted that they leave from London that very same afternoon. And Sarina had been in no position to argue. About anything.

Obedience did not come naturally to her, but she'd bitten her tongue, ducked her head—metaphorically, anyway—and done what was asked of her while that horrible video played again and again in her head. Matteo had ordered her things brought from her hotel. Then he'd ushered her into one of his cars, settled in the spacious back seat beside her, and informed her that they would be driving up to his family's stately home in Yorkshire.

Sarina was sure that he'd been waiting for her to react badly to this pronouncement, so, naturally, she hadn't. She'd nodded and smiled in her best rendition of the kind of obedient creature she wasn't, and wondered how the hell she was going to make it through this ordeal.

Especially when being close to this man made her behave like someone else. Someone who *touched* men for absolutely no reason and when it was the very last thing she should have been doing under the circumstances.

What were you thinking? she asked herself for the nine hundredth time that minute as the car wound around and around the desolate hill toward Combe Manor.

But of course, that was the trouble. For the first time in her highly academic, resolutely intellectual existence, she hadn't been *thinking* at all.

And really, she'd expected him to do…*something* on the way to this village in Yorkshire. To taunt her, at the very least. Stick his knives in deeper. Or do whatever it was he'd done in his office that had made her act the way she had. Like a completely different woman had inhabited her body when he'd touched her.

Sarina had steeled herself as she'd settled on the wide leather seat, certain she wanted nothing to do with whoever that different woman was and *certain* she could *ward him off* this time despite her previous behavior—

But all Matteo had done was pull out his phone and some papers. And then he'd rolled one business call into the next for the entirety of the trip north, speaking at least six different languages, to her ear.

Instead of relaxing Sarina, because he wasn't paying her the slightest notice and no *warding off* was necessary, it had only made her more tense.

She had never felt like a pawn before. She had felt helpless and powerless when Jeannette had fallen into the clutches of the man who had ruined her, but Sarina had gone and built the rest of her life in deliberate response to that. Since then, she had always made sure that she was in charge. It was one of the reasons she had succeeded at her job for all these years. She was never off balance. She was always, always in control.

And she didn't know quite what to do now the tables were turned.

She didn't know…how to sit. How to hold herself. How to function when she knew Matteo pulled all the strings now.

She had never learned how to dance like the marionettes the British loved so much—and she wasn't sure she was ready to start.

It was late when they arrived at the manor house. Though it was lit up imposingly, the night itself was damp and shockingly, relentlessly dark. There were no stars to cast a little light and remind her that there was more to life than the comeuppance that awaited her within the grim stone walls of this place. And as Matteo ushered her in from the car, through the imposing front door, Sarina took in gulps of air that chilled her inside as well as out.

"Welcome to Combe Manor," Matteo told her, almost offhandedly, as he led her into the hall. "No one in its known, recorded history has ever been happy here, but who knows? Perhaps you will be the first."

Sarina eyed his forbidding profile, not sure how to respond to that. Not sure what to do with herself—or with this dangerous man who had showed her his teeth already. "It would be helpful if you set out the parameters of this arrangement."

"All in due course," he replied, sounding very nearly merry. And that glint in his gray eyes was downright festive. "Enjoy the dread and apprehension, Sarina. Those are two of your favorite weapons, are they not?"

And she couldn't say she much cared for the way his mouth curved as he looked at her, with something she would never be so foolish as to label a smile.

She wanted to fight. She wanted to do…*something*.

But he only nodded, and it took her a moment to realize it was to someone who'd materialized silently behind her. Because, of course, he had staff. Likely quite a lot of staff.

"Angela will see you to your room," he told her in that same merry way. "And I will see you tomorrow morning, bright and early. I can only hope you spend the night awake and staring at the ceiling, reliving your each and every sin and regret."

She started to reply the way she usually did, sharp and cutting in return, but stopped herself.

"Look at that," Matteo murmured, with a kind of dark approval in his voice that made everything inside of Sarina…slide around, hot and bothersome and wrong in every possible way. "You can learn. I am so proud."

And then, when he waved his hand like a king to a peasant, she had no choice but to follow the silent, notably unfriendly Angela through the great, echoing house as she was bid.

Everything he'd said to her had sounded like a threat, and echoed there inside of her, growing. Expanding. Making it harder and harder to breathe.

She assumed that had been his goal. And she would have died before admitting it to him. Sarina hardly wanted to admit it to herself.

She was deposited in a suite of rooms that looked out into the thick night off the back of the house. Or so she assumed, as she couldn't see even the faintest light to suggest a village down below. Perhaps in the morning she would see fields. The famous moors, perhaps. But tonight there was only her own reflection.

And the last person Sarina wanted to look at was herself.

She took a shower, hoping the hot water would soothe her, but it didn't help. She climbed into the big, canopied bed that stood against one wall in the bedroom, turned off all the lights, and lay there.

Staring at the ceiling, just as Matteo had predicted, wondering how all of this had come to pass. Not only what had happened earlier in his office, with that video—and her own out-of-character reaction to him. But…everything. Her life.

How had she ended up in this gloomy old house,

more or less a prisoner of a man she'd hated on principle alone *before* he'd hoisted her up high on her own petard and let her swing?

You know how, that voice inside of her that she was beginning to hate along with Matteo Combe, chimed in.

And she might not like to admit it, but she did know.

Sarina had started off with the best of intentions. She'd mourned Jeannette through her work, and she'd honestly believed that she was doing good. She had always prided herself on her research, and had stood up to many a board of directors who she'd determined were unfairly targeting their executives, usually because someone was jockeying for position. She'd been pleasantly surprised many a time. And when necessary, she'd taken a certain pleasure in ridding the corporate world of terrible, selfish, narcissistic bullies who were only vulnerable to their bottom lines and the men who controlled it.

She had been ethical, always, or so she'd thought.

But somehow, somewhere along the way—and it pained her to admit this to herself—she'd turned into the enemy herself.

And it had taken Matteo Combe, of all people, to make her realize it.

By the time the dawn crept in, light gleaming at the edges of the curtains she'd drawn tight, Sarina had tossed and turned the whole night through. The way he'd told her he hoped she would, which made the hollow feeling inside her ache. Her eyes were gritty, she felt scraped raw, and she had spent the night obsessively going over each and every case she had ever had.

She knew she hadn't been wrong about the men she'd helped topple from their exalted positions. They had been noted bullies. But that didn't make Sarina herself the bright, shining light of righteousness she'd imagined herself all this time.

Her motivations weren't quite as noble as she'd thought they were, were they?

Because she couldn't help thinking that if she was a truly good person—if she'd honestly tried to help Matteo, say, instead of going out of her way to push him over a cliff of her own making—she wouldn't be here.

About to face her own reckoning whether she wanted to or not.

She rose from her bed, feeling like a very old woman. Every one of her joints seemed to ache as if she'd developed a terrible arthritis in the night, so she went and sat in the tub for a while, hoping that hot water and a liberal application of the fancy bath salts she found next to it would do her some good.

But when she got out, she smelled rather strongly of lavender and was otherwise unchanged.

A different maid was waiting for her when she emerged from her bedroom.

"Mr. Combe would like to see you now," the girl said, and when Sarina tried to smile her thanks, it was as if she was wearing a mask of her own face. Her mouth didn't seem to work any longer.

She'd tossed on the clothes she usually saved to wear when she was blissfully alone in her hotel room—a pair of comfortable, stretchy trousers and a soft pullover. She thought about changing into something more professional, but discarded the idea. There was no point putting on any kind of armor. Not now. Not when she had sunk so far.

And more, not when Matteo would know exactly what she was doing and use it against her, as she had to believe he would.

She didn't even bother putting her hair up into its usual smooth twist, which was her version of a white flag of surrender. She followed the maid down the hall as she was, then down the great stairs. The house was quiet all around her, and filled with as many shadows as fussy statues and ponderous art.

Sarina was halfway toward thinking the whole manor house was a kind of stuffy museum to dead people, like most of Great Britain to her mind, until they turned a corner and arrived at a surprisingly sunny little breakfast room. It sported a view out the bay windows of rolling moors in the distance, brooding and beautiful, and an exquisitely manicured garden closer in, and worst of all, there at the table with his dark gray eyes already glittering with more victories she knew would cost her, was Matteo.

Her doom.

And if she was brutally honest with herself, her just desserts.

"You look sufficiently martyred," Matteo said, that dark voice of his cutting through all those voices and regrets in Sarina's head. "I half expected you to walk into this room dragging a crucifix behind you."

There were several propped up amongst the hideous artwork cluttering up the second floor, she nearly said, but caught herself. That was old Sarina. New Sarina was more circumspect.

She stood where the maid had left her, there before the table where Matteo sat, as if awaiting his judgment. She forced her neck to bend, clasped her hands before her, and tried to appear demure.

Whatever that looked like.

"Are you unwell?" Matteo's voice was a dark lash. And if she wasn't mistaken, that was amusement in his gray eyes. "You're looking rather peaked."

"I am perfectly well," Sarina said. And then, because perhaps there was only one Sarina and she had no idea what she was doing, she smiled.

"Well rested, in fact. I'm not sure I've ever slept so deeply in my life."

His eyes were like smoke and they laughed at her, though he made no noise and his stern mouth did not curve in the slightest. "I'm delighted to hear it. The manor house is not known for its hospitality, much less its comfort, but it thrills me that you again defy expectations."

He had not invited her to sit, and if this was any other day, Sarina would have pushed it. She would have gone to the table and helped herself to his seat. Then to the coffee she could see steaming away in the French press at his elbow.

But she didn't dare do any of those things, because she couldn't help thinking this was all a test. One that was set up for her to fail already.

So she stayed where she was and endeavored to look totally at her ease.

"I thought stately homes such as this were meant to be the first word in comfort and hospitality." She worked on her smile, aiming it at him and trying to imagine it without edges, somehow. "Surely that is its purpose."

"How delightfully American." He sat back in his chair, folding the paper he'd been reading in front of him, its pink pages gleaming faintly in the sun. "You misunderstand entirely the purpose of a pile of stones like Combe Manor. Comfort and hospitality are the very last thing one should expect from a place like this. It is a monument to cold, hard ambition. Each and every stone represents a chunk of human soul given or traded away by one of my ancestors. There is only one way to rise from peasant roots to wealth like this, and it isn't a pretty road. The house is meant to cause nightmares, not dreams. Some might call it a cautionary tale."

"If you dislike it so much, why come here at all?"

"Because it is my home, Sarina. Whether I like it or not."

He studied her for a moment that dragged on too long, then nodded to the chair opposite him.

She didn't wait for him to clarify his feelings about his home. She sat down, and tried not to sigh audibly when he filled her coffee cup for her. And she knew that he was likely doing it to sneak beneath her defenses, put her off her guard—but she didn't care. Not when there was coffee.

"Last night you wanted parameters," he said as she took her first deep sip, the rich, strong brew shooting through her, right where she needed it. "There is only one thing I want. You need to convince my board that my behavior is above reproach. You must give them whatever reports they need to prove that I am not merely the best CEO and president Combe Industries has ever had, I am, indeed, the best of men."

Sarina took another pull from her coffee while

she tried to collect her thoughts. "Do you think that will work?"

"If it does not, you and I will both be out of a job, and I suspect that video will make the nightly news."

Just in case she was tempted to forget where she was. And why. No matter how great the coffee was after a restless night.

"Yes, thank you. I haven't forgotten that you're blackmailing me."

"I prefer to think of it as an inducement to do the right thing."

"The right thing, in this scenario, being perverting my methodology to produce the result you want. On command."

"Are we pretending that you walked into your first meeting with me without an agenda in place?" Matteo's voice was silky then, but that only made the blade of it slide in deeper. "How can I pervert a methodology that is already twisted and biased?"

Sarina cleared her throat, and did not answer that. "Normally how this works is that I take a full month to six weeks. I have as many meetings with the subject as I deem necessary. After each meeting, I routinely check in with my client and tell them how I think these meetings are going."

"Have you checked in with them after your meeting with me yesterday?"

She didn't want to think about yesterday at all,

and certainly not when she was in his presence. But that was one more thing that wasn't up to her anymore.

"No."

Matteo nodded at her and she thought she could see every San Giacomo ancestor of his in the way he inclined his head, as if he was too noble to live.

She assured herself she found that repulsive. But the slick heat between her legs told her otherwise, and she didn't know what to do with a disobedient body. It had never happened to her before.

"Go on then," he said, a silken order. "I want to listen to your report."

She hadn't expected this, and she should have. Sarina couldn't understand how this man kept catching her off her guard at every turn. What was the matter with her that she couldn't seem to get her bearings around him?

Even as she thought it, she felt her hand twitch, and she knew that if she'd been any closer to him, that hand would have reached out of its own accord to touch him.

Again.

She wanted to cry. She wanted to crumple into that broken heap she had been only once, after Jeanette, and had vowed she would never be again.

And that was the least forgivable thing in all of this, she thought. She could shrug off the blackmail as one more corporate manipulation, and call it even, really. But this man kept making her feel things she had been certain she had locked away forever.

Pain, hurt, helplessness. She thought she'd excised it all, but here it was again. As if it had been lying in wait all this time.

"Very well," she said calmly, though her tongue felt thick in her mouth. And she hadn't had near enough coffee. "If you insist."

There was the faintest suggestion of a smile on his lips then. "I do."

Sarina felt like she was having an out-of-body experience, except both versions of her were trapped here in this brooding house. With Matteo. And there was nothing for her to do but reach into the pocket of her trousers and pull out her cell phone, as he'd commanded.

She tried to school her features to the sort of impassivity that was called for here, but she couldn't quite get there. His gaze was too intent. Too dark and knowing.

She scrolled through her contacts, found the name of the chairman of his board, and pressed the button to call the number.

And as it rang, she stared across the table in all the surprising Yorkshire morning light, wishing that something—anything—could dull the man in front of her. This was the first time she'd seen him in natural light. No rain outside to mute the impact he had. No clouds or gray skies to make him less vivid.

Matteo was beautiful.

He wore dark trousers and a button-down shirt, open at the neck, as if he thought a business meeting might break out at any moment. He looked pressed and perfect, and the quiet exquisiteness of his clothing only underscored all of that brooding masculinity that seemed to wrap around her where she sat.

He seemed bigger now. Taller somehow, though the only thing that had grown since yesterday was her appreciation of his ability to play all the games she did, but better.

She set her teeth, cleared her throat as she heard the other line pick up, and then it was time for her performance.

"Speaker," Matteo mouthed at her, tapping the tabletop to underscore his command that she let him hear both sides of this call.

She obliged, of course. What else could she do? She pressed the requisite button, then set her phone down on the tabletop between them.

"I trust you're calling with more good news," came Roderick Sainsworth's booming voice. He had been Eddie Combe's best friend, and something of an uncle to Matteo and Pia if the reports were to be believed. But with Eddie gone, Matteo's scandalous behavior at the funeral presented

Roderick with an opportunity. Sarina understood men like Roderick completely.

If he kept it up, she would likely be hired to go after him next.

If all you're doing is playing whack-a-mole with sociopaths, that voice inside chimed in, *then why do it at all? You're not doing any good. You're just choosing one bad man over another. What's the point?*

But this was not the time for unpleasant self-examination.

"I dropped in on Mr. Combe unexpectedly last night," Sarina said in her usual clinical tone, which it only now occurred to her was awfully close to *bored.* That felt like another body blow, and she struggled to keep going. "As I explained to you at the start, drop-ins are an important part of this process. While it is always interesting to see what can be found out in the planned sessions, drop-ins force a loss of control. I prefer to conduct them in places where the subjects usually feel the most safe and inaccessible. That way the loss of control feels more like a personal violation. Which can often reveal a subject's true character."

Across the table from her, Matteo's gray eyes gleamed, promising a kind of retribution that would leave her breathless.

Assuming she could ever breathe again to note the difference.

"Yes, yes," Roderick huffed. "I remember the sales pitch."

"Mr. Combe responded as expected," Sarina said, and found herself unable to look away from Matteo. It was as if he held her tight in one of his fists, his grip unbreakable and fierce. Her eyes felt suspiciously bright, but she ignored them. "He was on the defensive initially, but then, to my great surprise, he rolled with the sucker punch."

There was a short silence on the other end of the phone. "I beg your pardon?"

"I found him rather agile, in fact, as he switched course," Sarina said, as if she was musing through the problem as she sat there. As if the man in question wasn't glowering at her from across a notably small table in a deserted room, high on a hill in a house out of a horror movie. "Some men rise to prominent positions through bullying, as I'm sure you're aware. Others ascend to those positions thanks to exactly this sort of agility. Their ability to pivot no matter what is thrown at them in the course of a day. It strikes me as a possibility that your Mr. Combe is the latter."

"If you're talking about his ability to pivot into a fistfight that makes the papers, perhaps," Roderick snarled. "I'm not paying you to let the boy turn your head."

Sarina stared across the table at the man before her, who only a very great fool would consider a *boy* in any sense of the term. She could see that darkness in his gaze, but otherwise he didn't so much as twitch. She looked for any kind of telltale sign that he was furious, because she could feel that he was, but there was nothing there. He might as well have been one of the stone gargoyles that graced his own roof here, theatrically snarling, but as still as the stone from which they'd been carved.

"I was under the impression that you were paying me for an assessment of your CEO and president following the events at his father's funeral," Sarina replied coolly, because she was regrettably not made of stone. "If your requirements have changed, Mr. Sainsworth, you will need to update me. But I should warn you right now, the assessment is the assessment. My head will not be turned by Mr. Combe, or you."

Roderick blustered on, claiming she'd misunderstood him, and Sarina continued on when he finished, presenting the man with a fairly nuanced picture of Matteo. But a positive one, at the end of the day.

And when she hung up, Matteo's mouth curved in her direction.

"Nicely done," he said, and yet somehow, a compliment delivered in that voice of his felt nothing like a compliment at all. "Presumably, as time goes on, you will get gradually more and more... enthusiastic." That word felt like a slap. She was instantly tossed back into his office, melting into that kiss—and she could feel her cheeks heat. Especially when his lips quirked. "The more you are captivated by my suitability for my job, of course."

"It will only take one more session," she told him, ignoring the heat on her face as best she could. "I always present my preliminary finding after three sessions. If that finding is that the subject would be better off removed from his position of power, we conduct a further set of sessions, to be sure. Usually three or four, depending on the situation."

Matteo studied her until Sarina was fairly sure her face would simply remain that hot. Forever.

"Out of curiosity, how many times have you gotten to the third week and pronounced one of your subjects perfectly able to continue his command of his company? Or do you find only guilty men wherever you look?"

"Guilty men are guilty," Sarina said as calmly as possible, though she felt as if that grip of his was tightening around her. "I don't make them that way."

"How remarkably convenient for a woman who makes her living pronouncing that guilt."

Sarina took her time draining the rest of her cup of coffee. Then she refilled it, cupping it in her hands as she leaned against the rigid back of her chair. She forced herself to meet that knowing gaze of his head-on.

"What, exactly, do you want from me, Mr. Combe?"

"Matteo. Mr. Combe was my father, and you are already aware of how I behaved at his funeral. Keep calling me by his name, and who knows what I might do?"

"Matteo," she said, and couldn't help but feel as if that was a surrender. His name on her lips felt distressingly intimate. But she tried to ignore that the way she was trying to ignore everything else. "You have what you want. You are in total control, and in a few days, I will call in with the results of your third and final session. I will sing your praises and we can be on our way. Yet I get the sneaking suspicion that's not enough for you."

"We must while away the intervening days in some fashion or other," Matteo said after another long moment of silence that tore at her. "I find I am desperate to understand you. While you slept so well and so deeply last night—" the look he sent her then suggested he knew exactly how she'd spent her night "—I searched for more information on Sarina Fellows, the avenging angel of a doctor who does not help people, but rather chooses her targets and takes them down. One by one."

She couldn't feel the expression on her own face, her cheeks were still so hot. "I don't have targets, I have subjects. And I only take them down if they deserve it. Some would say that taking those men down is a form of helping others all its own."

"I have no doubt that is what you tell yourself. But I want to know *why*."

Sarina directed her attention to her coffee again. "Because it's the right thing to do."

This was unbearable. And yet, thanks to that video, she had no choice but to bear it. She had no choice but to sit here and subject herself to whatever conversation Matteo chose to have, with her or at her. She was stranded here in this house of his, so far away from everything. But it wouldn't have mattered if they were smack down in the middle of a London street. A thousand people could be thronged around her, and he would still have had total control.

Because she'd given it to him when she'd lost her mind and touched him.

If he wanted her to talk about herself, something that Sarina had gone out of her way to avoid for years, she would have no choice but to oblige him.

Even if the words stuck in her throat.

Because how could she make anyone understand what Jeannette had been to her?

Sarina's friendship with Jeannette had blossomed into being when they were still in strollers, both in the care of nannies while their parents worked. Sarina's parents rarely left their universities. Jeannette's rarely came home from their medical practices.

Sarina and Jeannette had been left to fend for themselves, and they'd done it together. They became each other's family. In time, it was as if they were the real family and their parents were just afterthoughts. Footnotes.

Her own time in therapy while studying for her degree had forced her to face head-on how damaging this must have been. Even if she'd never felt damaged, not while Jeannette had been alive to make everything their very own adventure. How could she consider herself damaged when parental neglect, however benign, was the reason she and Jeannette had considered themselves blood—with the scars on their palms to prove it?

Girls with attentive parents didn't make blood oaths of enduring sisterhood at ten. And Sarina didn't want to imagine who she might have been if she hadn't been there that afternoon, with a sharp knife and all that giddy laughter up in the attic in Jeannette's house, ripping up old T-shirts to use as bandages.

But how did she explain that to Matteo, who had a real blood family and, if the photographs she'd studied were to be believed, had actually spent time with them?

Especially when he was already studying her like she was an animal in a zoo. "And you are certain that yours is the path of the righteous, are you not?"

She didn't believe that silky, almost-playful note in his voice. She didn't believe that he was anything but the danger she knew him to be. *She knew it*. And even so, his voice seemed to curl around inside of her, too hot and too intense.

Too dangerous by far. But there was nothing she could do about it.

"I am," she made herself say, and something broke inside her as she said it.

He wanted her to feel like the villain here, but she wasn't. *She wasn't*—or she hadn't been. Not every man in a position like Matteo's deserved to be pushed out. But each and every one of them could do with some serious, unflinching attention paid to the kind of men they were, or they became monsters. That was what she'd always believed.

All Sarina had ever wanted was to pay them that attention, the better to weed out those monsters before they did too much damage.

And she might not understand why she responded to this man the way she did, but that didn't mean she had the wrong idea about him. He was blackmailing her, after all. She might need to re-examine her motivations, but she had nothing to feel guilty about.

"I am certain," she said, and she heard that familiar spark in her own voice. The fire that had motivated her all these years.

I have nothing to feel guilty about, she asserted, deep inside.

"I understand," he said, and he sounded almost kind.

And Sarina could sense it then, the trap he'd laid for her. She might not understand where or how he would spring it—but she knew it was there. It was that hint of kindness when she knew there was none of that here. She knew it was part of the snare.

Especially when Matteo smiled. "Tell me then. Who is Jeanette?"

CHAPTER SIX

HE WATCHED THAT name strike her as if he'd hauled off and thrown a fist.

And it was a fist he'd meant to throw, so Matteo didn't understand why the sight of Sarina taking that blow made him... Uncomfortable. There was a part of him that still felt, no matter what, that he recognized her somehow and it seemed connected to the tightness in his chest.

But he ignored it.

Before him, Sarina had gone still. Pale.

"Jeanette Maroney lived next door to you as a child. You and she were fast friends, by all accounts."

"Sister."

Sarina sounded like someone else. Her voice was ragged, like a scrape through the surprising spring brightness of the breakfast room, the only tolerable room in this dark and stuffy house when the sun was out. Which in Matteo's memories of his childhood was never.

He didn't know why he tortured himself by coming back here when he'd always hated the place. Or why he was thinking about his childhood at all when he had this woman off balance before him. At last.

"I am not following you, Sarina."

She cleared her throat. She dropped her head and breathed out so he could hear it. And when she lifted her eyes to his again, there was something like defiance in her dark gold gaze.

Which should have annoyed him, not hummed in him like fire. Like need.

"She was my friend, yes. Always. But as far as I was ever concerned, we were sisters. She was my family."

"Would you like me to tell you what I found out about her?" Matteo asked, and had to remind himself that he need show no mercy here. That if she'd had her way, Sarina would have shown him less than no mercy in return. She'd never had any intention of walking away from this job of hers without his head on a platter.

There was no reason that he should find this difficult. That the sight of her in some kind of distress should make him feel…anything at all. Much less that stiffness in his own chest.

"I already know everything there is to know about Jeanette," Sarina said after a moment, and he could hear how tight her voice was, in contrast to that matter-of-fact tone she usually used. He could see how stiffly she sat there on the other side of the table. "I doubt very much that a recitation of events I lived through, picked up from a few internet searches and twisted to suit your narrative here, is going to tell me something I don't already know."

Matteo studied her face, and chose not to acknowledge the fact he'd already committed her every feature to memory. Just as he chose not to think too hard about how excited he'd been when he'd stumbled over those old pictures online the night before. The pictures that had led him down a dark rabbit hole to the sad, brief life of one Jeanette Maroney.

And her best friend, who had found her, and had spent the rest of her own life avenging Jeanette's loss.

"We appear to have found your motivation," Matteo said, almost idly. "The reason you spend your days in interchangeable hotel rooms, plotting out how best you will ruin the life *du jour*."

Sarina gazed back at him for a beat. Then another.

And then she laughed.

It was the first sign of life he'd seen in her since she'd shuffled into the room looking off balance and subdued, and the effect on Matteo was electric. He felt that laughter everywhere. And the fact that she sounded slightly unhinged did nothing to ease the hit of that electricity or the way it seared into him.

Had he thought he wanted to crush her? Because the truth was, he liked her this way. Alive and uncontrolled. Careless and bright with it.

Reckless, something in him whispered, as if passing down a dire sentence.

Because *reckless* was for other people. Never Matteo. Never the heir to two august families and their attendant fortunes.

But it turned out, he liked the sound of it in that laugh of hers.

"You should see your face," she said, and her eyes were far too bright as she shook her head at him, that recklessness all over her the way he wished he was. "You are so certain that you have me all figured out, aren't you? You know Jeanette died, and boom. There is my motivation. There's your psychological profile all worked out for you."

"A simple yes or no would do," Matteo replied coolly.

She laughed again, and he didn't understand what it was about that laugh that got inside him, and made everything… Messy. And not the kind of mess he knew how to clean up. Not the kind he'd spent his adult life learning how to handle.

This was the kind of mess that sank in deep. And stayed put.

"Jeanette was more than two dates and a dash on a gravestone," Sarina hurled at him, her eyes still too bright. And a different kind of intensity all over her face. "She told the worst jokes I've ever heard in my life. Deliberately. She didn't need music to dance, not that she had any rhythm, but she didn't need that, either. She was so smart and so gullible, all at the same time. And she was always late. Even if you told her to meet you at an earlier time than necessary, still. She'd find a way." She paused, a faraway look on her face then, as if she was remembering being kept waiting somewhere. She swallowed, hard. "Jeanette never met a stranger. She was relentlessly kind to everyone she met. Which isn't to say she was a saint. She loved drama. She would marinate in it. And she didn't get to grow old enough to learn how much better it is to live life with a whole lot less of it."

Matteo didn't recognize the feeling that swept over him. It took him too long to understand that it was a kind of shame, and he couldn't say he cared for it in the slightest.

"Sarina…"

But she didn't hear him. Or she didn't care if she did. "At first she didn't tell me about the new man in her life. Jeanette liked her secrets. She loved fairy tales more than anything, and when she finally did tell me that he existed, you would have thought she'd met Prince Charming. That was how she thought of him, of course. He swept her off her feet, wining and dining her all over the world, giving her expensive gifts, making her feel like a princess." Sarina was smiling then, as if she was telling a happy story, but there was that sharp brightness in her eyes. And besides, Matteo already knew how it ended. "Then she got pregnant. And there was no more wining or dining or fancy trips to far-off cities. He told her to handle it, cut her a check as some kind of final gift, and stopped taking her calls or making himself available."

"I assume he was married," Matteo said. "Isn't that usually how this story goes?"

"He had three ex-wives at that point, but he was never considering Jeanette for that role. And don't defend him to me," she said, her voice getting fierce, as if he'd argued that the man's marital status excused his behavior. "Not every man is cut out to be a father and emotions run high when there's an unplanned pregnancy. I understand that. But that doesn't give a man the right to be cruel. To be despicable."

Sarina took a deep breath, as if to steady herself, and Matteo wanted to tell her to stop. He didn't need to know the details, surely. What had he thought there was to gain in this? But he didn't say a word. And he didn't know if that was because he thought she wouldn't stop telling this story if he told her to, or if he was far more concerned that she would.

He looked at Sarina and it was as if he recognized her more than himself.

And he didn't know what on earth to do about that. So he did…nothing.

And Sarina squared her shoulders, looked him straight in the eye, and kept going. "He ordered her to get rid of the baby, and when she refused, he relented. She thought her determination to win him back had worked. She thought that, as she'd suspected, a little time had made him realize that *of course* he wanted his own child. He took her out to dinner, made love to her, and told her everything she wanted to hear." Her voice cracked a little there, but she still pushed on. "But he was gone when she woke up in that penthouse suite at the Four Seasons. Bleeding all over the pristine, high thread count sheets."

Sarina reached out for her coffee then. She picked up her cup and took a sip, her motions stiff and jerky. Almost like a robot, except there was still that terrible storm in her eyes that told Matteo she was anything but a machine.

You wanted to see who she was, something in him reminded him harshly. *Now you know.*

"Jeanette didn't understand. She called him to let him know what had happened. That she was miscarrying the baby he'd spent the night before assuring her he wanted after all. And do you know what he did?" Matteo could guess. But he found he couldn't bring himself to say a word. "He laughed at her."

"Sarina," he started again. This time, she lifted a hand, and it only occurred to him after he subsided that she wasn't the one giving the orders here. That he was supposed to be.

But there was that ribbon of shame still bright and hot inside him, reminding him he'd forced her to tell this story—and what did that make him? Was he any different from the self-interested bastard she was telling him about now?

Matteo had the uncomfortable notion that it was nothing but a matter of degrees.

"He laughed at her, called her an idiot, and told her exactly what he put into her drink the night before. So then she called me." Sarina's gaze was locked to his, grief and fury and something else he couldn't name blazing there. It made that shame inside him bloom into its own kind of fire. "I came, collected her, and brought her home. And that's why I was there to find her the next morning, after she'd taken every pill in our medicine cabinet, and then, just to make sure, used her razor on her wrists."

There was nothing but silence between them then, there in the too-bright glare of the temperamental Yorkshire sun through the windows, and a dull beat that it took Matteo long moments to realize was his own heart.

Kicking at him hard. Demanding to know how exactly he had become the kind of man who would force a woman to tell him a story like that. Who had come into this meeting gleeful at the notion he had *ammunition*.

When, exactly, had he become his father? And how had he failed to notice that appalling transformation before now? He had loved the man. He had admired his effectiveness, even. But he didn't want to *be* his father. Something he'd been a lot clearer about before Eddie had died, making Matteo's desire to be his own man feel like a betrayal.

But there was no time for that quagmire, not while Sarina was still gazing back at him. All that she'd lost stark and clear on her face.

"So, yes," she said, all the tears she hadn't shed there in her voice. "You could say I had a vendetta against that particular man. But a funny thing happened while I dedicated myself to his downfall. I met all these other men who seemed a whole lot like him. And as satisfying as it was to ruin a man who destroyed the best friend and only sister I ever had, I thought that I could do real good in the world if I prevented other men from doing the same thing to women just like her. Which I think you're well aware, many of them do."

She didn't say, *you do too*—but that was what Matteo heard. Another hint he'd become Eddie Combe after all.

"That is a horrific story," he said, hoping his voice sounded smoother than the riot inside him. "I apologize for throwing it in your face."

"I don't need your apologies," Sarina threw right back at him. She stood then, rising to her feet with a certain grace that made him even more appalled at himself. At what he'd become when he'd thought he'd spent the whole of his life making certain he could never, ever turn into his father. *Never.* And no matter the twinges of disloyalty thinking that caused. "I brought this upon myself. If you want your pound of flesh, go right ahead and take it." But her gaze slammed into his like a blow. "Just leave Jeanette out of it."

"I don't understand," his assistant said through the phone much later that day, and though her voice was scrubbed clean of any particular inflection the way it always was, Matteo could see her dubious expression as clearly as if she was standing in front of him in the library at Combe Manor. Instead of down in his London offices, holding down the fort the way she did so beautifully. "You thought you'd go ahead and punish her by…spiriting her away to the family estate for a bit of a refreshing holiday?"

"I'm handling Sarina Fellows," Matteo told Lauren, his own voice shorter than he'd like. "I have something else entirely I need you to do."

"If you mean you need me to run this office in your absence, I can assure you, sir, everything is handled exactly as you'd prefer it."

"I have no doubt," Matteo said. He never doubted

Lauren. She took efficiency to the level of art. "This is something a little bit different."

It had been a long, strange day. He had started the morning focused and more than ready to tear strips off Sarina. But that wasn't what had happened. He had pushed her, and she'd told him more than he ever wanted to know about her lost friend—and about her, really, in the process.

He'd been left in that breakfast room thinking he didn't know who the hell he was anymore.

Or worse, he did know.

When Matteo really had spent his life trying his damnedest to learn from his father, yet never become him.

It had been impossible not to love Eddie. Or his only son had certainly found it impossible. Eddie had always been larger than life. As embarrassing as he was refreshing, often all at once. Brash, pugnacious, in-your-face Eddie Combe had been a force of nature. There was no small part of Matteo that couldn't believe, even now, that something as prosaic as a heart attack could have taken Eddie out. When he'd thought about his father's death, as he had done a great deal in his periodically angry adolescence, he'd been unable to imagine anything less than an act of God doing the trick. A biblical flood, pointed directly at Combe Manor. A hurricane for one.

Anything less, surely, and Eddie could have fought it off the way he did everything else.

But instead, poor diet and indifferent exercise had worked in Eddie the way it did in any other mortal man.

Matteo had always taken his father's behavior as a guide—and, often, as a cautionary tale. He exercised all the time. It was his favorite and only habit, if he was honest. He watched what he ate. He tended to his body as if he expected to live forever, because that was his plan. He didn't do business the way his father had, a handshake one day and a cudgel the next. He used logic. Reason. And a certain pragmatism he'd honed at Cambridge, the London School of Economics, and the many years he'd worked in Combe Industries, in every single position he could, so he knew his inheritance inside out. The people and the positions alike.

Unlike Eddie, who had swanned about like he was the king of the world, issuing orders and laying down the law on a whim because Eddie had trusted his own gut above all things.

Matteo had admired that as much as he'd despaired of it, which was as good a way as any to describe his relationship with his father.

It hadn't been until this morning that he'd stood in this house where generations of Combe men before him had raged through the halls, bullying the servants and browbeating their families, that

Matteo understood that despite his best efforts, he was no different than any of them.

He might not have raised a fist, but he'd had no compunction whatever when it came to throwing emotional punches at Sarina. He had *wanted* to take her down. His urge for revenge had consumed him ever since she'd sat in his villa in Venice and had dared to act as if she had power over him.

That was what had led him to poke at her grief, just as his father would have done before him. All gut, no logic.

Matteo didn't quite know how to live with that.

He had been the one who'd left that breakfast room, walking out without another word and leaving Sarina to stand there alone, very much as if he couldn't face her for another moment.

That bright current of shame inside him had suggested he couldn't.

Because he was terribly afraid that facing her meant facing that ugly part of himself that was his father after all—that had always been his father, waiting there inside him—and he'd wanted nothing to do with it.

But it wasn't as if he could escape himself. Especially not in this house, this repository of generations of bad memories. His ancestors had been so certain that they could buy their happiness once they made their money, and one after the next, they'd learned that wasn't the case. They could

SPECIAL EXCERPT FROM

✦HARLEQUIN

Presents

To avoid destitution, Luli needs outrageously wealthy
Gabriel's help. The multibillionaire's solution? He'll
secure both their futures by marrying her! But sweeping
Luli into his luxurious world, Gabriel discovers the
chemistry with his untouched wife is priceless...

Read on for a sneak preview of
Dani Collins's next story,
Untouched Until Her Ultra-Rich Husband!

You told me what you were worth, Luli. Act like you believe it.

She had been acting. The whole time. Still was, especially as a handful
of designers whose names she knew from Mae's glossy magazines behaved
with deference as they welcomed her to a private showroom complete with
catwalk.

She had to fight back laughing with incredulity as they offered her
champagne, caviar, even a pedicure.

"I—" She glanced at Gabriel, expecting him to tell them she aspired to
model and should be treated like a clotheshorse, not royalty.

"A full wardrobe," he said. "Top to bottom, morning to night, office to
evening. Do what you can overnight, then send the rest to my address in
New York."

"Mais bien sûr, monsieur," the couturier said without a hint of falter in
her smile. "Our pleasure."

"Gabriel—" Luli started to protest as the women scattered.

"You remember what I said about this?" He tapped the wallet that held
her phone. "I need you to stay on brand."

"Reflect who you are?"

"Yes."

"Who are you?" she asked ruefully. "I only met you ten minutes ago."

"I'm a man who doesn't settle for anything less than the best." He
touched her chin. "The world is going to have a lot of questions about why
we married. Give them an answer."

#3725 A SCANDALOUS MIDNIGHT IN MADRID
Passion in Paradise
by Susan Stephens

A moonlit encounter tempts Sadie all the way to Alejandro's castle...and into his bed! But their night of illicit pleasure soon turns Sadie into Spain's most scandalous headline: *Pregnant with Alejandro's baby!*

#3726 UNTAMED BILLIONAIRE'S INNOCENT BRIDE
Conveniently Wed!
by Caitlin Crews

To prevent a scandal, Lauren needs to find reclusive Dominik—her boss's estranged brother—and convince him to marry her! As Dominik awakens her long-dormant desire, will Lauren accept that their hunger can't be denied?

#3727 CLAIMING HIS REPLACEMENT QUEEN
Monteverre Marriages
by Amanda Cinelli

Khalil's motivation for marriage is politics, not passion. Yet a sizzling encounter with his soon-to-be queen, Cressida, changes everything. And the desire innocent Cressida ignites is too hot to resist...

#3728 REUNITED BY THE GREEK'S VOWS
by Andie Brock

Kate is stunned when ex-fiancé, Nikos, storms back into her life—and demands they marry! Desperate to save her company, she agrees. But what these heated adversaries don't anticipate is that their still-smoldering flame will explode into irresistible passion...

COMING NEXT MONTH FROM

◆HARLEQUIN
™

Presents®

Available May 21, 2019

#3721 THE SHEIKH CROWNS HIS VIRGIN
Billionaires at the Altar
by Lynne Graham

When Zoe is kidnapped, she's saved by Raj—an exiled desert prince. The attraction between them is instant! Yet her rescue comes with a price: to avoid a scandal, Zoe *must* become Raj's virgin bride...

#3722 SHOCK HEIR FOR THE KING
Secret Heirs of Billionaires
by Clare Connelly

Frankie is shocked when Matt, the stranger she gave her innocence to, reappears. Now she's in for the biggest shock of all—he's actually *King* Matthias! And to claim his heir, he demands Frankie become his queen!

#3723 GREEK'S BABY OF REDEMPTION
One Night With Consequences
by Kate Hewitt

When brooding billionaire Alex needs a wife to secure his business, his housekeeper, Milly, agrees. But their wedding night sparks an unexpected fire... Could Milly—and his unborn child—be the key to Alex's redemption?

#3724 UNTOUCHED UNTIL HER ULTRA-RICH HUSBAND
by Dani Collins

To avoid destitution, Luli needs outrageously wealthy Gabriel's help. The multi-billionaire's solution? He'll secure both their futures by marrying her! But after sweeping Luli into his luxurious world, Gabriel discovers the chemistry with his untouched wife is *priceless*...

His words roused the competitor who still lurked inside her. She wanted to prove to the world she was worthy to be his wife. Maybe she wanted to prove her worth to him, too. Definitely she longed to prove something to herself.

Either way, she made sure those long-ago years of preparation paid off. She had always been ruthless in evaluating her own shortcomings and knew how to play to her strengths. She might not be trying to win a crown today, but she hadn't been then, either. She'd been trying to win the approval of a woman who hadn't deserved her idolatry.

She pushed aside those dark memories and clung instead to the education she had gained in those difficult years.

"That neckline will make my shoulders look narrow," she said, making quick up-and-down choices. "The sweetheart style is better, but no ruffles at my hips. Don't show me yellow. Tangerine is better. A more verdant green. That one is too pale." In her head, she was sectioning out the building blocks of a cohesive stage presence. Youthful, but not too trendy. Sensual, but not overtly sexual. Charismatic without being showy.

"Something tells me I'm not needed," Gabriel said twenty minutes in and rose to leave. "We'll go for dinner in three hours." He glanced to the couturier. "And return in the morning for another fitting."

"*Parfait. Merci, monsieur.*" Her smile was calm, but the way people were bustling told Luli how big a deal this was. How big a deal Gabriel was.

The women took her measurements while showing her unfinished pieces that only needed hemming or minimal tailoring so she could take them immediately.

"You'll be up all night," Luli murmured to one of the seamstresses.

The young woman moved quickly, but not fast enough for her boss, who kept crying, "*Vite! Vite!*"

"I'm sorry to put you through this," Luli added.

"*Pas de problème.* Monsieur Dean is a treasured client. It's our honor to provide your trousseau." She clamped her teeth on a pin between words. "Do you know where he's taking you for dinner? We should choose that dress next, so I can work on the alterations while you have your hair and makeup done. It must be fabulous. The world will be watching."

She would be presented publicly as his wife, Luli realized with a hard thump in her heart.

Don't miss
Untouched Until Her Ultra-Rich Husband.
Available June 2019 wherever
Harlequin® Presents books and ebooks are sold.

www.Harlequin.com

make money, and by God they did, but happiness was far more elusive.

The library Matteo used as his office when he was up north was a perfect example. It was a beautiful room, featuring a skylight far above and glorious bay windows with the view of the village below and the hills in the distance. The bookshelves were evenly spaced and filled with gleaming, leather-bound books.

Except none of the books were real. The spines had been painstakingly crafted to look like real books, but inside, the pages were blank and empty. It had been important to his great-great-grandfather to appear as educated and worldly as the men he wished were his peers, but Geoffrey Combe hadn't been one of them.

That was the curse of families like Matteo's. They could rise. Money was buoyant, after all.

But they could never, ever wash off the stink of their humble beginnings.

And the more Matteo had sat there, ignoring all the calls he should have been making as he stared at those fake books before him, the more he'd come to understand that they weren't simply a funny little anecdote about long-dead men. They were him.

He had all of those San Giacomo genes, sure. He looked the part. But inside, where it counted, he was blank straight through.

And the sheer horror of that realization was why

he determined that it was high time he behaved in a way he knew his father never would have. And hadn't, in fact, when given the opportunity.

"There was a part of my father's will that I haven't known quite what to do with," he told Lauren now.

"Shall I read it and tell you what I think you should do?" she asked, in her usual matter-of-fact way, because that was what she was paid to do. Know him better than he knew himself, and act in his stead when necessary.

He didn't ask her if she knew how blank he was inside. He didn't think he wanted to hear her answer.

"This is somewhat trickier," he said. "It seems my mother had a child before she married my father. And she left him the bulk of her fortune in her will."

And Lauren proved her worth all over again by not reacting to that bit of news in any audible way.

"Why hasn't he come forward to claim his fortune?" she asked instead, quite sensibly.

"Two reasons," Matteo said. "First, as far as I can tell, no one is sure how to find the man. The last anyone heard he was in a forest somewhere."

"A forest," Lauren replied, her voice dry. "That narrows it down considerably. Was that all the information your mother had?"

Matteo didn't want to talk about his mother. He

hadn't wanted to talk about her when she'd died so suddenly. And the six weeks that passed before Eddie had died too hadn't changed anything. Alexandrina had mixed her wine and painkillers one night in a manner everyone assured everyone else was purely accidental, and Matteo had accepted that.

Alexandrina wasn't a box Matteo wanted to open. Because he had no idea what else he would discover about himself if he rummaged around in his mother's life—or her death. That he was crippled from the pain of losing the mother he'd never known well?

Or that he wasn't?

"Second, and more importantly, the request was left in my father's hands," he said, as if he hadn't heard Lauren's question. "But it did not appear that he intended to honor it."

"I see," Lauren murmured.

Matteo did not tell his assistant his fears that he had already gone too far down the road to becoming his father. He didn't explain why that was something he didn't want, just as he didn't try to pretend what he already knew. That it was entirely within character for Eddie Combe to ignore information he didn't want. Like the fact that Alexandrina, the San Giacomo wife he had worked so hard to win, had been possessed of a life, a history, and indeed, a son, before she'd met him.

"I need you to find him," Matteo said instead. "By whatever means necessary. He is a member of this family, and whether he chooses to stay in his forest or not, it should be a choice *he* makes."

Not a choice yet another angry member of the Combe family made for him. Whoever he was.

And the fact he had a brother only a few years older than him was something Matteo intended to hold deep inside himself. Not quite a scar, not quite a pleasure, but both at the same time. Or neither.

But at least it was better than the blankness.

He put down the phone, aware of that same edgy restlessness that had plagued him all day. As if his skin was two sizes too small. As if his bones no longer fit the way they should.

As if he really was one of these collections of empty pages masquerading as a book, and now he knew it, he could feel nothing but the falseness of it. Those ornate covers pressing down hard on the emptiness within.

Making him a stranger to himself, blank straight through.

And it somehow made perfect sense that when he looked up, Sarina was standing in the doorway.

His very own avenging angel, with a sharp tongue in place of a terrible sword.

His trouble was, he still wanted to taste her.

CHAPTER SEVEN

SARINA WAS STILL in the same clothes she'd had on this morning, and now that he wasn't trying to tear into her, Matteo allowed himself to notice that what she wore looked soft and far more lived-in than the crisp black pieces she'd worn at both of their official sessions. And avenging angel or not, he couldn't help thinking that this was the *real* Sarina before him.

She looked…approachable, instead of sleek and intimidating. Touchable instead of bristling with all her deliberately sharp edges.

Not that thinking such things helped Matteo handle that wild, nearly out-of-control greed for her inside him any better.

She'd put her hair up, clipping it back from her face in the way he knew she liked. But all it did was draw more attention to her fascinatingly high cheekbones and her beautifully wide mouth.

And all he could think about was the fact he knew how she tasted.

"What brings you back into my lair?" he managed to ask when the silence had dragged out too long and still she stood there, not quite inside the library. As if she planned to turn and run at the faintest sign from him.

Matteo opted to flash that sign. He lifted himself from his chair as if they were facing off. As if this house was a boxing ring and as if, at any moment, he expected a fight might break out. He squared his shoulders like he was preparing to go a few rounds with her, and he didn't allow himself to remember each and every time he'd watched his father do the same.

Just as he didn't allow himself to think any further about how much of Eddie there was in him, especially around this woman.

"I expected you to make a break for it," he said instead. "It's an hour's walk into the village. Another hour or so to York to catch a train. You could have made it down to London by now."

Sarina's mouth curved, though if it was a smile, it made his chest hurt. And made that greedy thing inside him kick into higher gear.

He had to believe that whatever that said about him, it wasn't good.

But he couldn't seem to make it stop. Any of it.

"The story of what happened to Jeanette isn't new to me," Sarina said quietly, her dark gaze on

his. "I'm no more or less sad about her than I was when I woke up this morning."

"Good," Matteo heard himself say, and was struck at once by how scratchy his own voice was.

And how inadequate his response seemed, particularly as it hung there between them like smoke.

And he noticed too many things in the silence that stretched out across the library then. The light had changed over the course of the day as the typical clouds had crept in. Now that it was evening and the last of the sun was clinging to the horizon, all he could see in this library—in this house— were the shadows. Like creeping, deepening monuments to all the sadness that had gone on here and had pooled in him despite his best efforts, over the years, to make himself different.

Matteo didn't understand why looking at Sarina made it worse.

Or *more*, anyway. She made him feel more than he wanted to, or should, and he found himself rubbing at that space between his pectoral muscles where she had placed her hand, as if he could rub all those sensations away.

"What happened to you in this house?" she asked, as if she was there on the inside of his head when she was still standing in the doorway.

He disliked the sensation. Immensely.

"I don't know what you mean."

She folded her arms and regarded him steadily. "You do. You've made more than one reference to the fact that this is an unhappy place. Why?"

"Did you fail to notice where we were when we arrived?" He gestured toward the windows. "Or take a peek at the view? Textile mills and row houses as far as the eye can see, on both sides of the river. Smokestacks like steeples all over the Pennines."

"You said this house was the problem, not the mills in town."

"I admire that you imagine there could be some separation between the fate of the mills and of the people in this house. Outward appearances to the contrary, they have always been inextricably linked." His head tilted to one side. "I had no idea you were so interested in the history of the area. Why is this under discussion in the first place?"

"I was under the impression time was of the essence," she replied, and the more jagged and undone he felt, the smoother she sounded. It pricked at him. "The sooner I can report on a third session to your board, the sooner we part ways."

He had been thinking something similar earlier, when he was virtuously sending his personal assistant off to corral his long-lost brother, the better to distinguish himself from his father. But he found he didn't like it much when she said it.

"Because now, of course, we're in some kind of

a hurry. There was no sense of urgency whatsoever when you were in control of these proceedings."

"I thought that was what you wanted."

But she didn't say it in any kind of obsequious fashion. There was something in that gaze of hers that struck him as wholly uncowed by anything that had happened. Whatever she said to make it sound as if his wishes were of concern to her, all she really wanted was to get away from this. From him.

Matteo shouldn't have cared what she wanted. He was the one blackmailing her, after all.

But he hated it.

God help him, but he *hated* it with such force he was surprised his skin didn't peel away from his bones. It felt as if it might.

"I am beside myself with astonishment," he found himself growling at her, as if he was suddenly unable to play this game he'd set into motion himself. What was *happening* to him? "My wants and needs are suddenly of paramount importance to you, the woman who wished to ruin me. Oh happy day."

"I must have misunderstood you," Sarina replied, almost sweetly. Almost. "Do you want to wrap up the current situation with your board of directors and return to your regular life unscathed? Or do you want to toy with me, playing cat and mouse games in this empty old house of yours?"

He considered her. "Must I choose?"

She shifted where she stood, her chin lifting in a wordless display of her defiance, even now. Even here. "Don't feel you need to rush to a decision on my account. But I'll remind you that every day that passes with this cloud over your head, your ability to lead your company effectively becomes more questionable. Still, I suppose you must do you."

That scraping restlessness inside him crystallized, turning into something else, brittle and bright in turn.

"This is not a happy place," he said, his voice gruff. And all this maddening woman did was gaze back at him, as if she wasn't the problem. "It is filled with ghosts of desperate, determined men who got some of what they wanted, but never all. And worse still, the women and children they took their disappointment out on."

"I thought the Combes were rich industrialists, stretching back generations."

"Some of them were. And they enjoyed being rich, do not mistake me. But naturally, when a man gets most of what he wants, he spends his time concentrating on what he cannot get. In my family's case, that would be acceptance into society. Believe you me, there is nobody more desperate than a rich man who wants to be an aristocrat, but can never wash away the taint of his peasant blood."

"Surely your father broke this tradition for you. He might have had *peasant blood*—" and she said those words in that uniquely American way, infused with the brash certainty that theirs was the only classless society in the history of mankind "—but he married into an aristocratic Italian family. You should therefore be happily untainted, shouldn't you?"

"My parents' relationship was a famous love story." Matteo couldn't stand still. He found himself roaming across the floor, not meaning to end up in front of her. Not conscious that was what he was doing, anyway. But then there he was "Do you know what that means?"

Sarina shrugged, which seemed particularly provocative when he was this close to her. "Thinly veiled made-for-cable movies based on their lives? Or more likely, on intrusive articles about their lives?"

Matteo smiled and thought she saw the warning in it when her expression turned wary.

"Mostly what it meant was that they were focused entirely on each other, to the exclusion of all else. Who was faithful. Who had lied and about what. Who had flirted at this or that party the night before. They betrayed each other a thousand times a day, fought, fell apart, and argued their way back together. Over and over and over again, always conscious of the fact that any misstep they made

would be seized by a greedy public and dissected by strangers. They were deeply concerned about those strangers and only occasionally forced to notice that there were other people in this house. Children, for example, who might need or want the occasional hint of parental affection. But children are not the storytelling public, forever obsessed with other people's fairy tales, so we were usually ignored."

Sarina's gaze searched his. "That doesn't sound like a love story at all."

"What is love if not the stubborn insistence that hope must vanquish experience, time and time again, despite all evidence to the contrary?"

His own cynicism seemed to have a scent, acrid and thick.

But it was true, so there was no reason he should have wanted to gather those words up, take them back, keep her from hearing them. Much less the echo of them, filling up the room all around them.

"You should think about opening up your own line of sentimental greeting cards," Sarina suggested after a moment. Her voice was dry, her chin was lifted, but once again, that too-rapid pulse in her throat gave her away. "Just think of all the money you could make with all that…unnecessary emotional honesty."

"My mother called my father a bully. My fa-

ther called my mother deceitful. They both would have called their relationship tempestuous. But I will tell you, as the child who was forever buffeted around in the storms they kicked up between them, I just wanted them to be the people I thought they were. A man too mighty and a woman too beautiful for the world."

"But it was the house you blamed. Not them."

"Some say there is a curse." Matteo was closer than he should have been. Standing over her in that doorway, every part of him focused on Sarina, as if her upturned face was causing that bright, brittle shattering inside of him. And he couldn't say it *wasn't* her. Nor did he step back. "No one who's lived here has ever been happy, so the locals mutter no one ever will. Even the ghosts are too depressed to get in a good haunting."

But he felt haunted anyway. He'd felt it since she'd walked into his villa and turned his life on end. She was his only ghost, and the closer he stood to her the more he felt that same tug of reluctant recognition that had dogged him since he'd laid eyes on her.

It didn't escape him that she did not appear to be similarly afflicted.

"Do you think that being raised by people who were forever at odds in this way affected how you behaved at your father's funeral?" she asked, in case he'd had any doubt on that score.

"Why are you psychoanalyzing me, Doctor?" Matteo's voice was so low it was barely a lick of sound, though it felt much louder inside of him. "We are past that now, are we not?"

"I have to follow a certain protocol," Sarina replied, and then swallowed, hard, that pulse in her neck telling him that even if she wasn't haunted the way he was, she was still affected. That was something. He told himself that had to mean *something*. "The third meeting requires a presentation on my part to the client."

"The client who is not paying you to find me a sympathetic figure and will likely take against you when you do."

"Whatever outcome Mr. Sainsworth may want, he is actually paying me to be impartial. You heard me tell him so myself."

"Is it believable, do you think?"

And something in him broke then. He couldn't seem to keep himself from reaching out when he knew he shouldn't. When he knew it not only told her things he should want to keep from her, it put him in the same position she'd found herself in yesterday.

Yet he still let his finger do what it liked, tracing the line of her jaw, then dipping down to move back and forth over that pulse of hers. Until he could feel the beat of it deep in his own sex.

"You are feared for your takedowns, not your

support. How will Sainsworth react when the feared enemy of the C-suite actually…suggests a CEO not be fired?"

She reached up and grabbed his finger. To stop him, presumably.

Though he was perverse enough to feel it like a caress.

"You threw Jeanette in my face for a reason." Sarina's voice was quiet. It seemed to shudder its way through him—something he liked about as much as he did that steady, knowing gaze of hers. "And I didn't like it, but I understand why you did it. It's far more upsetting to face the fact that you have a point. While I've always prided myself on my impartiality, it's possible that I've allowed myself to assume guilt rather than allowing the facts to lead me to the appropriate conclusion, whatever that might be."

Matteo didn't make the mistake of imagining she was complimenting him. Much less surrendering. Or, heaven forbid, apologizing.

The way you rushed to do, a snide voice inside him supplied. Unhelpfully.

That smile of hers was still razor sharp. "But we will never be able to tell whether my mandated glowing report on you is something you actually deserve. Or whether it's simply the spoils of war because you managed to outmaneuver me."

"Something I can live with, I think. As it hardly matters."

"It matters to me." She pushed his hand away, and he let her do it. But only so he could watch, fascinated anew, as she drew herself up taller. "I don't necessarily need your life story, Mr. Combe. But the more detail I can give that shows we really did have a third session, the better. You understand that it's not just your professional reputation on the line."

For the first time in his entire life, Matteo didn't care in the least about his professional reputation or how it made him like or unlike his father. He should have moved back. He should have continued his restless pacing around the library, since he couldn't seem to stay still. But he didn't do either one of those things.

"I understand that I asked you to call me by my name," he said instead, watching her pulse tell him the truths she wouldn't. "That you won't begin to feels like deliberate provocation."

"I think that might be some leftovers from your parents' relationship, maybe floating around here like your ghosts," she shot back at him. "It shouldn't matter what I call you."

And he thought about the books, the damned books, volume after volume with nothing inside them. All those leather covers, crafted to show-

case a wealth of knowledge no one in this house possessed.

And somehow that tangled around inside of him, kicking over into this woman, her taste, and the fact he hadn't felt like himself since she'd walked into his villa in Venice.

He was terribly afraid he never would again.

"It seems to me you should be far more concerned about keeping me happy than you are," he pointed out, as if he hadn't spent the day questioning himself. "I would have thought that was the point of blackmailing someone, if I'm honest. Built-in genuflecting, bowing and scraping on command, I would have said."

"I was under the impression your specific blackmail threat was about sex and shame," she hurled right back at him. "Bowing and scraping weren't mentioned."

"Surely that part was implied."

He didn't expect it when she jerked forward, her gaze bright with something it took him too long to realize was a kind of fury. On the surface, anyway.

But when he did, his body responded instantly. Hard. Hot. Ready.

"The fact of the matter is that you're just as bad as any other man I've taken down," Sarina informed him, very distinctly—as if to make certain he was paying close attention. "The funny part is that *they* all knew exactly who they were.

You're the one who seems to be confused. Let me clear that up for you. Good men don't blackmail. The end."

"Good women don't build their lives around revenge fantasies," he hurled right back at her. "So I will thank you not to imagine you are somehow cantering about the moors on any kind of moral high horse."

"I have a purpose. My life has meaning. It doesn't have to make sense to you, or anyone else. It doesn't have to be right." She threw each word at him as if she thought she might cut him in half. He had no intention of letting her see how easily she could. "And I certainly don't care if my choices make overstuffed, overconfident men like you uncomfortable."

"The only thing you have going for you, Sarina, is my goodwill." Matteo laughed. Loud, because the only kind of *goodwill* he had about her concerned getting inside her. Before he exploded. "And here you are. Squandering it by the moment."

She rolled her eyes. At him.

"Your problem is that you're used to people being afraid of you. I'm not. I don't want that tape going out in the world, true. But I'm not *afraid* of you, Matteo."

He swept his gaze over her, noting the flush in her cheeks, the way her chest moved with the force of her breath, and even the fists she curled

her hands into at her sides. Curled and then un-curled, as if in time with that pulse in her neck.

The one that matched the answering pulse in his sex.

And somehow, he didn't think this was a sim-ple as her temper. But he could think of one thing that was resolutely simple. The most simple thing in the world.

"If you want me, Doctor, all you need do is ask."

The effect on her was instant. And electric. She stiffened, then her cheeks flamed.

"You pompous, conceited, insufferable—"

"Sarina, Sarina," he murmured, her name a con-fection in his mouth, sweet and right. "That is not how you say please."

CHAPTER EIGHT

"Or," Matteo continued, his voice silk and sex and too many other things Sarina didn't know how to name, though she could feel them all like velvet temptation inside of her, changing her, "perhaps you do not know how to ask for what you want. Is that it, little one?"

Sarina had already been angry. She had spent the day locked away in her rooms, going over what had happened in that breakfast room again and again. Better still, picking through every moment of every interaction she'd had with this man, still trying to understand how she'd ended up here.

How he could be so loathsome—to throw Jeanette in her face, to challenge her the way he did—and yet she still felt that molten betrayal pulsing between her legs.

It was worse now.

Much, much worse.

And the things he'd said to her made her want to

scream. Sarina gulped that down, but she couldn't seem to do a thing about the thick heat that burst all over her and kept right on going, making her... burn. As if she'd thrown open the door and stepped into a sauna and wasn't sure she could breathe through the steam.

"Don't call me that," she said. Because it was the only thing she could think to say. "I'm not your *little one*."

And her stomach dropped, because the look he gave her then was... Different. Considering. Pure male speculation mixed with something else, something that looked a good deal like...patience.

Patience etched on stone.

It made her feel as if he'd reached down inside of her, rummaged around, and turned her inside out.

"You were a very driven child," he said, his voice musing, which seemed to connect directly to all the heat that suffused her. "You were the valedictorian of your high school class. You excelled in college, maintaining a distractingly high grade point average all four years."

Of all the things she'd imagined he might say, it certainly wasn't that.

She tried to pivot. To follow him wherever he was going, the way she would have done if this was any kind of normal session. She was supposed to be good at this. Following the threads, knitting them together—

But he was talking about her life. And he was doing it with that odd light in his dark gray eyes, that *patience* she couldn't help but think boded ill for her, and worse still, she couldn't seem to catch her breath.

"I'm actually already conversant on my academic record, thank you," she managed to say, and she didn't understand why she felt shaky. When nothing was happening.

Except… She didn't feel right. She thought maybe she was coming down with something, brought on, no doubt, by the stress of all this. She felt weightless and raw, swollen and shaky, all at once. She was wet between her legs, her breasts actually hurt they ached so much, and she couldn't think what could cause all of those things at once. It had to be that she was coming down with something.

"You applied yourself with the same rigor to your graduate studies. And then you lost your friend."

"No one talks about her anymore," Sarina said quietly, despite how bizarrely ill she felt. She was sure it was an illness, though she didn't feel *sick*. Just…off. "Too many years have passed. Half the people I know now don't remember her, and those who do think too much time has passed to bring her up at all. It's like she never existed. Normally, I would be delighted that her name came up twice in one day. But you've managed to ruin that, too."

Something flashed in those stormy eyes of his, but his devastating mouth only curved. Almost gently, she might have said—if he was someone else.

Because she could handle almost anything from a man like Matteo except unsolicited glimpses of what she refused to consider evidence of his humanity. Anything at all but that.

"I am forced to consider the evidence, little one," he said then, and there was something about the way he used that phrase. *Little one.* It should have enraged her and Sarina assured herself it did—but really, what she felt was weak. As if three strange syllables had stolen her feet out from under her. "So much focus, determination, and drive. One close friend, lost too soon. No relationship since. Not even any stories of hard drinking in all those hotel bars you frequent. I am forced to wonder…"

Then he made everything worse. He reached over, threading his fingers through her hair, and tugging it out of the clip she'd fastened at the back of her head as if it was an inconvenience to him. She felt the mass of it fall around her shoulders, and she hardly knew where to look, as he wrapped a thick sheaf of it around one finger. Then tugged.

"Sarina. Dr. Fellows." His voice was a velvet scrape down the very center of her. "Are you a virgin?"

There was a ringing in her ears. And she knew, somehow, that it was connected to all the rest of her ailments. But she managed to arch her brows, meet his gaze, and even smirk a little bit. Because if the *Titanic* was going down, she might as well rearrange as many deck chairs as she could while it sank.

"Virginity is a very specific, pejorative patriarchal construct," she told him. "Even you must recognize that, I hope."

"You have either had sex, or you have not." Matteo's mouth was in that patient curve, and if sheer, male amusement was a scent he would have reeked of it. "Construct it or deconstruct it to your heart's content."

"I don't like that word. I don't believe in it." She lifted a shoulder, then dropped it, but she knew even as she did it that it was hardly the effortless example of how little she cared that she'd wanted it to be. Because everything inside her was too... *Sick,* she told herself. She was sick, that was all. "What a ridiculous unit of measurement."

"I believe that depends very much on the unit in question."

"Do you know who cares about things like virginity? Excitable preteen girls. And certain men who should know better."

But if he was listening to her, he gave no sign. "The particular unit, and if I'm being honest, the

man who wields it. And how. It is a talent, not a skill."

"I'm not going to answer that question," Sarina said, with a sniff. And she couldn't describe the look that moved over Matteo's face then, especially when he laughed.

"But you see, you already have."

Sarina pulled in a breath, ready to launch into another set of arguments, about something, anything—

But Matteo...picked her up.

It was like the world made sense one moment, and then in the next, she was drop-kicked into a parallel universe.

Where all she could do was feel.

His arms wrapped tight around her. That chest, hard and impossible and pressed against hers.

The crook of his neck, right there where her mouth wanted to go, and that scent of his surrounding her, making her wish she could bathe in it. Hard, hot male, with a certain spice that was entirely Matteo.

She let out a sound she didn't recognize as her own when her back came up against the wall.

He held her there, pressing into her as his hands worked to pull her legs around his waist.

"What are you...? What is...?"

She couldn't find the right words. The sentences didn't seem to work.

There was nothing but Matteo, hard against her. Everywhere.

And that almost-stern sort of knowledge in his gaze as he looked down at her. Stone and certainty, and it made her shudder in a different way altogether.

It made her wonder if she had wanted precisely this all along. If her body had known things she didn't since the moment she'd met this man in Venice.

"There are different ways to fight, little one," Matteo said, his voice rough and perfect at the same time, and all the better for being so close to her now. "Let me show you."

And he bent his head, taking her mouth in another kiss.

When she had barely survived the first.

This was different. Hotter. Wilder.

But it had the same effect on Sarina. It was like being struck by lightning, shivering straight into the hit, and then begging for more.

She stopped thinking.

She twined her arms around the hard column of his neck. She was delighted that he had already wrapped her legs around his waist, so she could clench them tight. She found the hard ridge of him in his trousers, and followed some ancient, feminine wisdom locked in her hips as she moved that molten, wet heat of hers against him.

And if she was sick, he made her sicker. And well at the same time.

Until she couldn't really tell the difference.

The only thing that made her breasts stop hurting was to hurt them more, deliciously, as she pressed them against his chest. He kissed her like he owned her—like he knew her, inside and out— angling his head from one side to the next until he found a better fit.

Deeper, darker and more intense.

And Sarina gloried in it.

If this was a fight, she had been waiting for it all her life. She threw herself into it. Heedless. Reckless.

She didn't care if he had an entire film crew set up across the room this time. She wasn't sure she even cared if he was broadcasting it live to the world.

She hadn't known that anyone could taste like this, dark promises of wild pleasure, male and right. She hadn't known that she could feel so bright and hot between her legs, and fit him the way she did, arching against him as if she'd come alive right here. Today.

Wrapped up in her enemy's arms.

God, the things she hadn't known.

He shifted, pulling his mouth from hers to drop it against her neck, where he lit new blazes and sent the flames dancing and spinning all over her body.

"Hold on," he advised her, and she thought he cursed then, some long string of Italian syllables that sounded to her like music.

She held him tighter, and he reached down between them, working his hand beneath the drawstring of her trousers.

He found the soft core of her easily, and then his hand was there where she needed him most, sliding into all her heat.

He did something with those fingers of his, hard and talented at once, and she caught fire.

She shook and she shook, and the world shook with her, and it wasn't until he was coming down over her, there on the thick, deep carpet where she'd ended up without her knowing, that she understood what was happening.

And she didn't care, because Matteo was braced over her, and then his mouth was on hers again, and she'd had no idea until today that anything could burn this much and keep right on going.

And she had never done this before, but that hardly mattered. She had always fought, and so she fought here, too.

To get closer. To taste him, everywhere, now that she knew what that was like. And how good he was against her tongue. He pulled her soft shirt over her head, then tossed it aside, so she did the same with his. He spread her out on her back, then found her breasts with his mouth, his

hands. Until she was arching into him, moaning out his name.

And when it was her turn to fight her way on top of him, she tasted every part of that impossible chest of his that she could find.

He stopped her when she made it down over the hard ridges of his abdomen, tracing her way toward the waistband of his trousers. He rolled away, kicking off his trousers as he went, so Sarina tugged hers off, too.

"You will be the death of me," he said in a low, dark tone, his voice so thick he hardly sounded like himself.

"Then we will become ghosts of Combe Manor, just like the rest," she told him, lit up from inside with some kind of ferocity she'd never felt before.

And she was the one who crawled on top of him, desperate to hurl her way back into that fire again.

He let her, laughing darkly against her mouth as she rocked against him. She was drunk on the feel of it, his flesh against hers, and she thought she could go on like this forever—

Until clearly, he'd had enough. She tried to focus on him and saw his mouth was that stern line again. And his gaze was like rain.

And the hands wrapped around her hips brooked no argument, not even one of hers.

He lifted her, then shifted, so she could feel the

hardest part of him, nudging up against the place where she was hottest. Softest.

"All you need do is take what you can," he told her, and his expression was as certain as his voice. She trusted him—something she had no desire to tear apart or look at more closely, especially not now—and more than that, she wanted him. This.

All of this.

She braced her palms on his chest, settled herself against him as best she could, and then slowly, slowly, took him inside of her.

There was a pinch. Or more a kind of scraping sensation, so she paused. But it went away again, and she kept on.

By the time he was fully sheathed, deep inside of her, she'd gone bright hot again, red and wild. Everywhere.

And she could feel all the tension in him, sharp and hot.

"Now what?" she asked, breathless and beside herself, and yet utterly focused on the man beneath her.

And the part of him that was inside of her.
Inside her.

"Are you in pain?" he asked, and though he sounded strained, she saw no hint of it on his face.

"I told you. *Virgin* is just a word."

"And not one that applies to you any longer," Matteo replied, his voice the kind of dark that

seemed to flood her, filling her up until she felt it everywhere. "And all you need to do now is move. However you like."

Sarina experimented. She rolled her hips. She lifted herself up, then moved herself back down.

And everything was more of that same fire. She felt powerful beyond measure, and yet soft and bright straight through.

And she didn't know when she stopped playing, and started panting, deep shudders working their way through her as she searched and searched for something…

"Sarina." His voice was harsh, but it only made her want him more. "Sooner or later, you must surrender. You must."

And she wanted to tell him she didn't know how. That she refused. That she didn't have it in her to surrender—

But then, when he reached down between them and did something marvelous, she did.

In a bright fireball of something too sharp for joy, too sweet for pain, that exploded inside her over and over and over again.

He flipped her over onto her back, bracing himself against her as he surged even deeper inside of her. Teaching her that quickly and that thoroughly the difference between playtime and passion.

She seemed to hit one peak, then hurtle straight on into another.

Then another still, until the room was filled with the sound of sobbing, and she knew it must be her.

Sarina didn't have it in her to care about that, either. Not when she was lit on fire and burning as if she would never stop.

And when he followed her over, into that same fire, the only thing she heard was the way he said her name.

When she found her way back to herself again, Matteo was moving.

He had pulled a soft throw from somewhere, draped it over her, then lifted her into his arms again. She nestled her face against his wide shoulder and wondered dreamily if it was possible to put all the different, swirling pieces of herself back together.

Or if she even wanted to.

Especially when she was fairly certain there were things waiting there she didn't want to look at directly.

Matteo carried her up the grand stairs, then down a hall she hadn't seen before. At the end, he pushed through a door into a set of rooms far more grand and glorious than hers, with the gleaming lights of the village down below visible through all the windows.

He didn't take her to the stately platform bed that dominated the whole of the bedroom, but car-

ried her instead into the bathroom suite adjoining it. He set her down on her feet, then waited until she was steady, which she wanted to tell him was unnecessary. But her mouth didn't seem to work the way it had before.

Then he let go and Sarina felt exactly how rubbery her knees were. She held on to the side of the huge tub with its sweetly sloped sides, and couldn't seem to do a single thing but watch as he filled it.

When the water was hot and steaming, he lifted her up and set her into the water, then made her heart flip over inside her chest when he followed her in.

Matteo settled down against one sloping back of the tub, and she did the same, facing him, their legs tangled together in a casual sort of intimacy that made her heart skip a beat.

And suddenly, all the things she ought to have remembered seemed to buffet her, rising like the steam between them, making her think—

"Stop." Matteo's voice was harsh, the way it had been when he was deep inside her. And she shuddered as if he still was. "The world isn't going anywhere, Sarina. No need to invite it into this bath, I think."

She frowned at him, but he was moving again. He plucked her up, shifted her around, and settled her so her back was to his chest.

And Sarina had been holding on tight for the whole of her life. First to acquit herself well academically, as the only child of two intellectual superstars who barely noticed she was alive. Then there had been Jeanette, and she'd held on to her lost friend, the sister of her heart, even harder. She'd nurtured that tight grip. She built her life around it.

It had never occurred to Sarina to let go.

She would have said she didn't know how.

But here, plunged deep in hot water that felt like silk against her skin, Matteo hard and hot beneath her and around her, she felt herself... Open up.

And for once in her life, she didn't overthink it.

She let go.

It was the light that woke her, too bright when she always preferred to close her curtains tight against the very hint of dawn. It was the only way to handle the inevitable jet lag she suffered while she followed misbehaving corporate executives around the world.

She never, ever left her windows uncovered.

Sarina woke up with a frown, confused—

She felt him shift next to her in the wide bed, and remembered where she was in the next moment. And worse by far, who she was with.

Her eyes shot open.

And the reality of what she'd done slammed

into her so hard she was surprised she wasn't sick there and then.

It had been a very long night, like some kind of dream. She had let go in that bath, and then she had simply… Let it happen.

She'd leaned her head back against him in that tub, he'd taken her mouth, and then—eventually—he'd carried her from the water to the great expanse of his bed.

And they had stayed there while he'd taught her just how much it was she didn't know, and how delectable it was to learn it.

Over and over again, until she was limp and out of her mind, glutted on all that impossible sensation.

Sarina hadn't thought once about the fact this man was blackmailing her. The fact he held her entire future in his hands, or that she'd placed herself right there between his palms. Literally. And of her own volition. She hadn't considered the professional implications, particularly the fact she'd slept with a man who wasn't her client, but only because of a technicality. She was still supposed to be psychoanalyzing him.

She hadn't thought about any of that, and she certainly hadn't let herself think about all the ways she'd betrayed herself, and was continuing to betray herself, all through the very long night.

And worse, by far, she hadn't given a single

thought to how her presence in this man's bed meant she had thoroughly and completely betrayed Jeanette.

Jeanette, who had always told her that she couldn't understand why Jeanette had lost herself the way she'd done—but she would. Someday, she would.

Sarina felt her stomach heave, her heart kicking at her so hard and loud she was surprised it didn't wake the man still asleep beside her.

She eased herself to the edge of the bed, then slipped out of it. Outside she could see the first light hit the village, all the old brick buildings and narrow streets, then set the river to gleaming. She felt more than a little disoriented as she crept through the room, but she found that same throw he'd used when he carried her upstairs, wrapped it around herself, and tiptoed out of the master suite.

It took her longer than she thought it should have to find her way out of a wing of this house she'd never been in before, then all the way back down to the library. The clothes she was certain she'd left thrown on the floor were neatly folded on one of the chairs, reminding her that the staff, at the very least, knew exactly what she'd been up to.

That it was real. It had happened.

A suffocating shame squatted on her, fat and thick, as she pulled her clothes on.

And then she was moving blindly, racing back

up to her room, throwing her things into her suit-case, and heading for the door before she could think better of it. Or worse still, talk herself into staying. When she knew better.

When she had let Matteo Combe ruin her. When she had enthusiastically cooperated, in every possible way, with her own demise.

The sob that threatened to break free of her throat was too big. She knew if she let it out, it would take her down to the ground. Sarina held it in. Somehow, she held it in.

Just as Matteo had told her in his offhanded, imperious way, it took her a solid hour to march down that winding road into the village, where she hired a taxi at a stand near the coach stop, asked to be driven to the city of York, and once there, waited in the old train station until she could board the next train headed south toward London.

Because she didn't know who she'd become in Matteo Combe's arms. She only knew that she could not possibly allow herself to be that woman again. *Wanton. Soft and yielding.*

Desperate for his touch. Desperate for *him.*

The kind of woman she'd never been—the kind of woman she'd looked down on, if she was honest—who gave herself body and soul to a man like him.

As if she imagined she could do something so reckless without suffering for it.

When Sarina knew better. She knew she would suffer for all that pleasure, sooner or later. She already knew how things like this ended. Where touching a man like Matteo would lead.

Straight on into tears and loss and despair.

Whether Sarina wanted it or not.

CHAPTER NINE

MATTEO KNEW HE was alone in the stately bed in Combe Manor, another part of his inheritance whether he liked it or not, before he came fully awake that next morning.

He rolled over, then ran a palm over the sheets where Sarina had slept. Or, to be more precise, had rested briefly in between addictive bouts of the wildest passion Matteo had ever known.

Beside him, the sheets were cool. Matteo flopped over onto his back again and rubbed his hands over his face, all the things he didn't want to think about flooding into him like the ghosts he never wanted to admit could feel a little too real. Particularly in a place like this.

He had never been a playboy. Unlike many of the men he'd known at university, or socially, who had grown up the way he had—with plump bank accounts and investment income and too many strains of aristocratic blood in their veins—he had never attempted to distinguish himself by the

notches on his bedpost. He had never drowned himself in women only to become jaded and careless. As he'd told Sarina once, he had always been archaic.

That wasn't to say he hadn't indulged himself.

But it had never been like this.

He had never felt so unlike himself. So out of control and very nearly maddened with the need to keep tasting her, keep sampling her, keep making her cry out his name…

He felt that need wash over him anew, making him hard and ready as if he hadn't spent the whole of the night drowning himself in her.

There was something about Sarina that kept him off balance, even when he was the one with the experience and she the innocent.

Innocent.

That word went through him like a shudder, deep and dark, roaring in him like something primitive.

And it took him long moments to accept that what he felt was possessive.

Deeply, extraordinarily, unutterably possessive.

Because he had been her first. He had taught her how to please him, and herself, in every way he knew. He had taken her again and again, and when he'd been certain she'd had more than enough, she had crawled over him in the dark and started the dance herself.

He had never felt anything like this in his life. Addicted. Obsessed. Fully and completely needy, to his horror.

As if he was nothing but a man, after all.

Matteo jackknifed up in his bed, rolled out of it, and stalked off into his shower. Surely the heat would clear his head. Surely the water would wash these bizarre sensations away before he stopped recognizing himself altogether.

But when he emerged from all that steam, water, and heat, he felt as edgy as he had before. As if she'd done more than take him into her body— she'd wrenched him open and into a different shape than before. When he'd been perfectly content with the shape he'd been in before, thank you.

This was supposed to be a cold-blooded interlude. She had made a business out of her thirst for revenge. He had happily blackmailed her in return. Why was it the only thing he could seem to concentrate on today was the soft noises she'd made when he'd been deep inside her, so lost in her he wasn't sure he'd known his own name?

Matteo dressed quickly, then headed downstairs to the library again. He avoided the breakfast room entirely. He sat there, surrounded by the gold-embossed leather spines of books that weren't books at all, and told himself he didn't care what was or wasn't inside them. There was no shame in remaining opaque. Just because the world had

gone mad and pretended to value transparency in all things—as curated so carefully from behind so many screens—that didn't mean he had to partake in the obsession.

All he needed to do was glance out the windows to remind himself that in some places, history still squatted down hard, its solid haunches keeping everything more or less just as it had been for centuries. Why did he imagine he was the Combe who could change that?

He cracked open his laptop, set his mobile on the table before him, and applied himself to his work with all the focus and fury of a man who had no intention of cracking open the various compartments inside himself and seeing what lurked around in there.

If his life had taught him anything it was that a person's internal life should stay where it was. Lest it turn into hurled statuary, tabloid speculation, and his lonely childhood.

The morning passed with intense negotiations, contract disputes, and discussions with vice presidents stationed all over the world. And every time Matteo was forced to defend himself—without seeming at all defensive—against the sly little whisper campaign Roderick Sainsworth had started, using Sarina and her usual findings as his evidence—he was grateful.

It reminded him who he was. Who he had al-

ways been. And why he had made that video in the first place.

As the day wore on and he didn't see so much as the faintest trace of Sarina, Matteo was sure he understood. It was that edgy, restless feeling he'd woken up with and hadn't managed to conquer yet. He didn't like it. He felt certain that Sarina, with her deeply held distaste for *men like him*, found it all even more offensive.

He might even have found it ever so slightly entertaining that she'd apparently locked herself away rather than face what had happened between them. But by the time evening rolled around, Matteo found he was far less amused. It had begun to eat at him that Sarina was *so* distraught by the events of the previous evening that she'd shut herself away rather than face it.

Or, more to the point, him.

He prowled through the manor house, his already-dim mood blackening further with every step. He moved past the forbidding portraits of his Combe ancestors, studying them as he went. They were hard men, each and every one of them. Dressed up in the fashions of the day and clearly attempting to look more like the nobility than what they were. Tough and determined. Capable of climbing out of the textile mills into this manor house, if not as able to alter the broad, northern accents that marked them as *less than,* forever.

Or so Matteo's father had always told him every time he'd smacked Matteo for letting slip the posh accent Eddie had paid for in all those fancy schools.

And Matteo doubted very much that any of his ancestors—like his burly great-great-grandfather who had clawed the family out of poverty with his own two hands and ingenuity to spare—would have much use for a descendent whose head was so filled with a woman that he couldn't quite see straight enough to walk down his own damned hall.

Matteo didn't like to think of himself in those terms. But what other terms applied?

Especially when he could feel his body betraying him as he stalked toward the guest suite where Sarina was staying. Readying itself. Hardening into pure need.

He gave a peremptory knock at Sarina's door, then pushed it open.

But she was nowhere to be found.

And it took him only a moment or two to understand that she wasn't simply out of her rooms, wandering about the house somewhere. There was no luggage. No sign, in fact, that she had ever been here at all.

He retraced his steps, his jaw clenched so hard he feared he might shatter a tooth.

"Where is Dr. Fellows?" he asked the first member of his staff he found.

"I thought you knew, sir," the woman replied, looking immediately uneasy, which forced Matteo to wrestle his expression under control. Or try. "She left. Early this morning. By foot."

And he would never know what he said in reply.

He waited until the following morning. Only then did he ring her, standing in the library where he had first tasted her innocence, staring out at the clouds and gray while the weight of Combe Manor and the mill valley below him seemed to crush him into pulp.

"Dr. Fellows," she said by way of greeting, as if she didn't know exactly who was calling her. As if she truly believed that she could usher them back onto professional footing that way.

Though now that Matteo had tasted her, he was forced to wonder if anything that had passed between them had ever been professional. At all.

"It appears you do not understand how blackmail works, Sarina," Matteo said when she was sure he could sound very nearly disinterested. Cool and calm.

At complete odds with how he felt. And God help him, he was sick to death of all this *feeling*.

"I thought we agreed on our terms," came her reply, icier by far than his. And he would have moved the mills and factories below him with his own hands if he could have seen her face then. If he could have touched her. "I saw no reason to lin-

ger. Or did you imagine that you could keep me locked up in that house forever?"

"I did not keep you locked up at all, quite obviously, or you would still be here."

That came out somewhat less cool and calm, but she ignored it.

"I plan to make my presentation to your board in a week's time," she said, much as he imagined she would discuss her travel arrangements. Or a shopping list. "I will add you to the video chat room. If, for some reason, you do not like my performance or feel more effort is required on my part, we can talk further."

Even the way she paused then was dismissive. And Matteo didn't understand that howling thing inside of him that wanted nothing more than to remind her how it had been. How she'd come apart in his hands, over and over and over again. How she had surrendered, and in so doing, had humbled him.

Changed him, even, though he still didn't choose to accept that.

"Do you feel we have more to discuss, Mr. Combe?" Sarina asked, her voice as cold as it was challenging.

"I think not," he replied, ice for ice.

He put down the phone, stared out at all that wet and cold, and told himself he felt nothing.

Nothing at all.

A week later, to the day, he sat in his London

office and watched as Sarina spoke with quiet confidence into a camera.

He knew she was talking about him—or the character of him she and his board and perhaps the ever-present paparazzi had created between them—but he couldn't seem to focus on that. A few weeks back he would have said there was nothing more important on earth than his role in this company, he would have laughed at the notion that he might shift his focus from it for the merest instant, and yet today all he could focus on was Sarina.

She looked flawless, which irritated him, as he remembered her with color in her cheeks and tears in her eyes. Slumped over him, her skin glowing, sweet and hot. Today her thick black hair was pulled back into a sleek knot. Her cheekbones were as high as he remembered them, her mouth as temptingly generous. She wore that relentless black she preferred, smiled only very coldly, and kept her hands folded in front of her on her desk.

Behind her were a set of bookshelves, and Matteo had no doubt that she had read each and every one of the volumes lined up there.

Because Sarina is real, something in him whispered. *It's you that is fake.*

Or a ghost, perhaps. Of all the lives that had

come before him and failed, time and again, to do anything but end in disappointment.

No wonder she'd run off. As if pursued by wolves, unable to leave behind so much as a note.

Even the man she spoke of now, the Matteo Combe who she claimed to have profiled so thoroughly, was fake. A creation of his will and her surrender.

"The longer Mr. Combe and I spoke, the more convinced I became that his behavior at his father's funeral had far more to do with his understandable grief over being orphaned so suddenly than any defect of character," she was saying. "It seems in questionable taste to exploit a man's weakness. Another sucker punch, you could say."

If Matteo didn't know better, he might have thought that she believed that. That she believed in him—and when had he wanted that from her, or anyone?

As far as Matteo could tell, Sarina was his one weakness in all the world.

The fact he'd exploited her for his own ends made him no better than his own father, which was another way of saying that Matteo's worst fears had come true. Fears which had always been at war with his affection for Eddie. And he had to sit idly by, here in his expansive office, and watch it as it happened.

And he thought he knew, now, why he felt that

spark of recognition every time he saw her, as if he'd lost her long ago and had only just found her again. Or it was more accurate to say that he was *afraid* he knew.

But he had never been much good at being human, and she wanted nothing to do with the man who'd blackmailed her, so what he knew or didn't know would stay in him. Like one more ghost rattling its chain, all noise and no impact at all.

Eddie Combe had been many things. But he had never been *ineffectual*. Matteo would have to live with that.

When Sarina finished her tidy, matter-of-fact presentation, the rest of the board muttered amongst themselves.

"I am satisfied in every respect and delighted we can put this chapter behind us," Lord Christopher Radcliffe said at once, there in the boardroom three floors down in a meeting that Matteo had not been invited to join. He raised a brow in Roderick's direction, across the gleaming table. "Roderick? I'm certain you must be as relieved as I am that your fears were unfounded?"

"It is as if a great weight has been lifted," Roderick Sainsworth gritted out.

He had made a power play and lost. Matteo should have felt like a god.

Instead, he wanted the one woman in the world

who hated him the most to look at him like he was a man, not a science experiment.

But she'd logged off after delivering her assessment, her part already played.

"Thank you, gentlemen," Matteo said when it was his turn to speak into his monitor. "I appreciate the concern for my well-being, and that of Combe Industries, that led to this little adventure in psychotherapy. And I am delighted that the good doctor has pronounced me wholly fit to continue running my family's company as intended."

And when the video link went dead, when everyone had disconnected, Matteo was left staring at a blank screen.

He told himself that he should be happy, goddamn it, because he had everything he wanted.

Every single thing, he told himself.

Again and again.

Because sooner or later, he was sure he'd start believing it.

One week led into two. Three.

Matteo focused on the company because it was all he had. And all he knew how to do.

It was up to him to make certain that no matter his board's flirtation with the idea of voting him out of office, he was fully prepared to take Combe Industries to the next level. To build on the family tradition, and better it however he could.

Which meant, as far as he could see, *not* being his father or any one of his Combe forebears.

Something he had already failed to do in his personal life.

The better to remedy that, he set out to personally visit every single office. All over the globe. No matter how remote, how small, or how ancillary.

Two months in, Matteo saw his half brother for the first time over a video link from London while he was visiting the Combe offices in Perth.

"I would have known you anywhere," he said as he stared at the man before him on his screen.

Dominik was tall and dark, with the same gray eyes they'd both inherited from their mother. He was far brawnier than Matteo, his dark hair almost too long and a kind of wariness on his face that suggested a certain level of physical prowess, but there was no doubt that they were related.

"Brother," Dominik had replied, his voice gruff and a gleam in his dark gaze that told Matteo that for all he might have been a hermit, he was in no way a pushover. "What a pleasure to almost meet you."

Matteo counted that as a perfectly acceptable family reunion.

"What do you mean you're not coming straight home?" Lauren asked, once Dominik had left her office. She actually scowled at him through the screen, rather than gazing at him placidly, the

scowl merely implied. It was a shift in his normally unflappable assistant. "What exactly do you want me to do with your long-lost brother while you're out there traveling the world, indulging this sudden attack of wanderlust?"

Matteo shrugged, happy that he was in Perth and couldn't have rushed back even if he'd wanted to. "Civilize him, Lauren. He is a San Giacomo. Teach him what that means before the papers shred him into pieces."

"With all due respect, sir," Lauren replied, in a tone that suggested she thought very little respect was due, after all, "isn't that a job only you could do?"

But Matteo was doing his job. He was living his job.

Because he understood it now, after these weeks on the road. There could be women to distract a man. Children to clamor for attention. Family and all their demands and complications.

But the company remained throughout all those petty human concerns. The company had come before him, and it would carry on after him, much like the San Giacomo villa in Venice. He was nothing but a steward, protecting what his ancestors had built to hand it over, intact and hopefully improved, to whoever came after him.

"We have a brother, Matteo," his sister, Pia, said on a call one day. She wasn't doing a good job of

concealing the hurt in her voice, which told him she'd seen it on the news. "I'd think you might have called to tell me that, specifically, rather than letting me find out with the rest of the world."

"I didn't tell you because I didn't know if he'd ever be found."

"You didn't call me after he was found. After he married your assistant."

"I thought you were calling to tell me your own blessed event had occurred," he replied rather than answering her. Because he didn't know how to answer it. Was he pretending none of this was happening? His parents' deaths. His new family configuration. Pia's march to the altar, conducted in private ahead of her impending motherhood.

His parents were gone, and he would never know either one of them better than he did now. He was no longer the eldest brother, the oldest San Giacomo heir, which had always been a major foundation of his life. And the little sister who had always looked up to him, the only member of his family he'd loved unconditionally, had her own messy life to handle as she saw fit.

And he stood high in an office building in Hong Kong and thought instead of Sarina.

"Family is messy," his sister said quietly after a long moment, rich with layers Matteo opted not to excavate. "Look at our mother."

"I would rather not."

And indeed, Matteo never had. Alexandrina had never taken an interest in the son she'd complained was too much like his father. Perhaps Dominik, the true firstborn son she'd surrendered, was the reason why. But that didn't change how distant she'd been throughout Matteo's life. Or how little he knew how to mourn her when he'd hardly known her.

"You try being forced to marry against your will," Pia suggested, a dark note in her voice. "I doubt you'd fare any better."

"Pia." Matteo had promised himself—and Pia—that he would not interfere in her personal life after the funeral. He ran a hand over his face. "Is this a cry for help?"

"Of course not." But she was quiet for a long moment. "Maybe it would have been kinder to leave our brother where he was."

"That's a decision he will have to make on his own," Matteo told her, because it was what he'd told himself. It was what he believed, no matter what.

"Fair enough," Pia said. "You should go home, Matteo. It's been too long."

But it took him another six weeks to even think about making his way back toward London.

And he made a purely business-related decision to stop off in San Francisco on his way.

"I must commend you on this personal touch campaign," his American attorney told him with

a broad grin, shaking his hand when they met in an upscale bar in the city. It was packed with businesspeople in their suits and on their phones, wheeling and dealing the night away. "Must be exhausting, but it's already reaping huge rewards. What a brilliant move, to spin that mess at your father's funeral into a harbinger for the new era of Combe Industries."

Matteo had read the articles. *A Combe with a heart?* they'd asked.

Because now he was seen as some kind of hero. A man who had defended his sister while they'd all grieved, then had taken it upon himself to undo his own father's bitter legacy with an unexpected round of personal connection.

It was exactly what Matteo had wanted.

And he felt nothing.

"I am delighted it is having the desired effect," he told his attorney, and tried not to take against the man's endless *grinning*.

He already regretted stopping here. He had been away from London too long; he knew that. And while it was nice that it was working to rehabilitate his image—and with it, the company's—this tour of his had actually been a huge miscalculation.

Because out there in all the far-flung corners of the planet, Matteo had found himself sitting alone in one hotel room after the next, reliving that night in Combe Manor with Sarina.

He had spent these months making love to a ghost.

Until he was more than a little afraid that he had become one himself.

And no matter how much alcohol he tossed back with grinning men in suits like the one across from him tonight, it didn't make him real. It didn't fill the pages of those books with words, sentences, stories. All it did was further emboss that fool's gold on their spines.

"Don't look now," his companion said. Matteo's back was to the door, and though he heard an uptick in the noise level around them, it wouldn't have occurred to him to bother to turn. "Here's an opportunity for you to prove, beyond a shadow of a doubt, how little that nonsense with your board affected you."

"I haven't thought about it in months," Matteo lied.

"No time like the present," his attorney replied, and he was no longer grinning. "Because I can assure you it's all anyone's thinking about right now, no matter if they haven't given it a moment's thought since. And if they haven't recognized you yet, they will."

Matteo followed his attorney's gaze, shifting to look toward the door that led out to the street.

There was a scrum of people, exclaiming in that way they did when they were performing politeness for the group.

You wouldn't know genuine emotion if it bit you, that voice inside him pointed out, sounding entirely too much like the psychiatrist he'd never wanted. *You're not one to judge.*

The wall of people shifted and suddenly, she was there.

Sarina. *Here.*

Matteo went still. Except for once, it wasn't ice that held him in its grip. It was much too hot for that. Too electric.

His attorney was still speaking, but he could barely make sense of the words.

Because she was *right here,* and this was why he had come, he acknowledged now. He had put himself in her city as if it was a test of fate—and he'd won it.

And he had been carrying her face around inside of him so long now he'd begun to tell himself that he was overestimating her in retrospect. That no one alive could be as perfect as he remembered her.

But if anything, he saw now, he had underplayed the intense kick of her beauty. And what it did to him.

The soft silk of her hair. That fine, delicate nose and her dark eyes. Her mouth, the line of her jaw, the pert thrust of her breasts and the—

His gaze, greedy to take in all of her after all these weeks, stopped short at her belly.

Matteo had spent hours that night learning every inch of her. He had particularly concentrated on her lush hips. Her navel. And the sweet slope to the molten heat between her legs.

And the last time he'd seen her belly, it had been flat. Not jutting out as it was now in a dress that emphasized its roundness.

It was as if a bomb detonated inside Matteo. He was shocked to realize that he remained in one piece.

One moment he was a man who traveled the world, carrying his ghosts within him in and out of hotels and offices, one bleeding into the next while he remained numb.

And in the next, he was alive.

Bright and blisteringly alive, with a rage so deep and so intense he was truly astonished there were not pieces of him scattered all over this bar. That the bar itself still stood. That San Francisco itself had not been razed to rubble.

He rose from his seat, no longer paying the slightest attention to his companion.

Then he was moving, the crowd seeming to part before him with no effort at all.

He kept his gaze trained on Sarina as if she might make a break for it. As if she might turn tail and race out into the night the moment she saw him—and it occurred to Matteo that he didn't actually know what she would do.

But he knew what he would do.

Sarina was talking to the group arrayed around her, nodding as if she was engaged in the conversation. But Matteo saw the precise moment she noticed him bearing down on her.

Likely because he was a bright blaze of righteousness aimed straight at her.

She broke off midsentence. And he saw a complicated series of emotions race across her lovely face, too many to name, though Matteo recognized one above all the rest.

Guilt.

Bright red licked at the edges of his vision. His heart thundered inside his chest, though he thought not even a full-scale cardiac event could change his course or stop him. Not now.

"Matteo."

His name was a whisper. Or perhaps a prayer for deliverance. But he heard her all the same.

"Dr. Fellows," he said, though he hardly recognized his own voice. "What a surprise. In more ways than one."

She shifted away from her group, waving them off, though she never took her eyes from his. Because she was many things, this woman who had tipped his life on its end and ruined him, but she was no fool.

"Matteo." Sarina cleared her throat. "The thing is—"

"I understand congratulations are in order,"

Matteo said, his voice a silken threat that should have torn down the building. And the whole block along with it. "And I'm betting if I put my mind to it, I could guess exactly how far along you are. Shall we test that theory?"

"Matteo, I really… I think—"

He didn't move and yet she cut herself off as if he'd flipped a table. And that rage in him beat on, so dark and so consuming he was surprised he could see anything at all through the betrayal. And all the other dark things he couldn't quite name.

But he could see Sarina. No matter where he'd gone, how long he stayed away, he could always see her.

Damn her.

"Sarina," he said, almost softly. Almost nicely. "Little one. I will never forgive you."

CHAPTER TEN

KNOWING THAT THIS day was always going to come should have made it better.

But it didn't.

Sarina couldn't catch her breath. She couldn't do a thing about the way her pulse kicked in, harsh and wild.

Matteo's dark gray eyes were ripe with thunderstorms that she could already feel inside of her. When he jerked his head toward the door, Sarina turned and led the way outside. Away from all these people who were likely already alerting the world that Matteo Combe and Sarina Fellows seemed far more connected to each other than they should have been.

Out on the street, the San Francisco night was cool, and far quieter than the bar behind them had been. Fog was already creeping in, swirling around with the shadows and clinging to the lights. Making halos out of headlights and making all this worse, somehow.

Or maybe that was Matteo. He looked taller, though she knew he couldn't be. His shoulders seemed broader. His mouth was a stern, furious line, and still she wanted to put her hand on him. She wanted to sink against him, limp and delirious, and let him carry her as if she weighed nothing at all.

Sarina hadn't known it was possible to *want* like this. It had been bad enough these last months. It had been like a nagging ache, the way she longed for him, and she'd lectured herself extensively on how and why she wasn't going to fall into the trap of sentimentality so many did. He was her first; that was all. That was *all*.

But now he was a great deal more than that.

And yet Sarina suspected that even if she hadn't gotten pregnant, she would still feel shaky and overwhelmed and needy at the sight of him. She had no idea what to do with that, when it said so many things about her she didn't want to face.

"Are you well?" he asked, gritting out the question as if it caused him pain. "And the…baby?"

Sarina swallowed hard at his hesitation. And then again when he actually said that word. *Baby.*

"I'm perfectly fine," she managed to say, somehow, though she was half-blind with emotion she didn't want to admit she felt. "The exhaustion and nausea have passed, thankfully."

"I am delighted to hear it."

Every word he spoke was like a blow. He lifted a finger and a car pulled up at the curb moments later. Matteo wrenched open one of the passenger doors, his dark gaze locked to Sarina's like he expected her to take off down the block.

She was ashamed to say she considered it.

"I understand that this is a shock," she began, trying to sound calm. At her ease. "It was a shock to me, too. But I don't think that's any reason to—"

"Sarina." He sounded almost…kind. It was terrifying. "If you do not get into this car now, I will put you in it."

She believed him.

Sarina told herself it was the threat of being manhandled that had her following his orders, but she was fully aware she'd been fantasizing about his hands on her only minutes earlier. And ever since she'd marched away from Combe Manor, for that matter, though she didn't like to admit that. Even to herself.

She climbed into the back seat of the car. And then sat there in the charged silence as he climbed in behind her, something in him seeming to vibrate. As if he truly was a storm about to break.

"I thought I had the stomach flu," she found herself saying as the car slid into traffic. The divider was up, separating them from the driver, and she told herself it was a confessional. A safe enough space, back here in the dark, if she ignored

the large man brooding at her from the other side of the leather seat. "You know how the viruses are these days. They linger on forever. That's all I thought it was. But it didn't go away, for weeks and weeks. By the time I finally went to a doctor, they estimated I was already three months pregnant."

"Did this estimate occur today?"

She managed not to cringe at his icy tone. "No. But—"

"But you felt no need to tell me. I can only assume that if I hadn't happened to be in that bar tonight, if I hadn't happened to see you with my own eyes, you would never have shared this news with me."

Sarina blew out a breath.

"I don't know what I would have done." He started to say something and she frowned at him. "Neither do you. I was getting used to the idea. I hadn't made any decisions."

"Do you imagine that is throwing me a bone, Sarina? You did not make any unilateral decisions about *my* child? How good of you."

That was so sardonic it hurt. And she didn't think she could do this. But she didn't see how she had any choice. Wasn't that what he was so angry about? The choices she'd thought she had to…not do anything?

She cleared her throat. "It's not your *child*."

She could feel him grow sterner. Harsher. "I

would advise you not to lie to my face and tell me I am not the father. That you happened to have lost your virginity to me and then cavorted your way across Europe in the same fateful week."

"It's not *a* child, Matteo," Sarina managed to get out. "It's twins."

And she had to turn and look at him when the silence seemed to echo.

He was staring back at her, an arrested look on his face. "Twins."

As if he had never heard that word in all his days.

"It's why I'm already so big." She waved at her belly. "To be honest, I can't really process it myself. Much less…"

"Much less share it with the father of those twins. I am aware."

She threaded her fingers together and scowled at them, which she figured was less aggressive than scowling at him. And her guilt at not telling him the moment she'd found out was lessening by the second the more he raged at her about it. Because what did she owe him, exactly? She would have told him eventually. Surely she would have.

"You were off traveling," she pointed out. "It's not as if we exchanged cell phone numbers."

"Because if we know anything about you, Doctor, it is that you are stymied in the face of seemingly unreachable men off doing their busi-

ness. You have no history of hunting them down and forcing them to speak to you at your whim, whether they want to talk to you or not. You certainly didn't assemble an entire file on me while you were plotting to strip me of my own company. However could you have found me?" His eyes blazed. "You did not want to find me. I doubt you tried."

She felt too hot. Much too hot, as if she might be sick again—but she knew she wouldn't be that lucky. "I would have."

The laugh he let out then was hollow. Raw. And Sarina was sure it left burn marks all over her.

"You can tell yourself any lies you like, but I saw the truth on your face when you saw me in that bar," he growled at her. "If you could have kept this a secret forever, you would have. Let us be perfectly clear that this is the person you are."

The injustice of that walloped her and she forgot to be careful with him. With the volatile tension stripping the oxygen from the air between them.

"Says the man who blackmailed me into sleeping with him," she snapped at him.

He turned then, shifting his big body so fast that she caught her breath in a kind of gasp. But he didn't touch her.

He doesn't want to touch you, something in her insisted. *You've made him hate you.*

And she couldn't have said why that made her

feel inexplicably distraught when really, it should have been cause for celebration.

"I will be the first to list my sins," he told her, his voice low and hard. "I don't need anyone to provide me with a hair shirt, as I have my own. I did not blackmail you into sleeping with me. If you cast your mind back, I think you will find that you are the one who put your hands on me first."

"I was a virgin."

"Happily, you don't believe in such patriarchal constructs," he retorted, hurling her own words straight back at her.

And that same *distraught* feeling welled up in her again, but it had shifted. It felt bigger, more wobbly. And was complicated by the fact he clearly remembered their short time together as clearly as she did. As distinctly.

Almost as if it was something else entirely. Something less tawdry.

"Let me explain something to you." And Matteo's voice was a silken ribbon of sheer fury that wound around and around her, then pulled tight. "I have spent my entire life trying not to mimic my father's worst impulses even as I admired his ability to get things done. *He* took what he wanted and damn the consequences. *He* would have reacted very differently to a woman he desired sneaking off the way you did. *I* chose to take the high road."

He belted that at her, as if he was truly astonished that she didn't recognize his great sacrifice.

"The high road?" She let out her own pale rendition of a laugh. "You can't be serious. I wasn't required to leave you an outline of my reasons for not wishing to wake up in your bed."

"You didn't simply leave my bed, Sarina. You escaped from my home, setting off down the drive like a fugitive. On foot."

"I didn't owe you anything. I still don't owe you anything, including an explanation."

He moved even closer, and her body was a traitor. It didn't care if she was angry with him. It didn't care that she had resolved, over and over again these past months, to pretend he had never happened to her at all. Women raised babies on their own all the time. Sarina had built up a sizable nest egg and she was more than capable of taking care of her own children. She assured herself of that at least fifteen times a minute.

But her body didn't care what she felt prepared to do. It wanted him.

It wanted him badly.

Here. Now. Anywhere.

"Keep lying to yourself if you must," Matteo seethed at her. "But do not expect that I will believe it, too. I was there, Sarina. I know exactly what happened between us that night, and so do you."

This would be easier, surely, if she could just get a breath, but that didn't appear to be on offer.

"I'm sorry if you let your feelings get involved." She raised her chin as his eyes widened in astonishment. Tinged with that same fury. "We should have discussed our terms. I would have told you how unlikely it was that I would feel anything at all for a man who threatened my livelihood and held that over my head."

She couldn't read the emotions that chased across his face then, one after the next. And what terrified her was how much she wanted to read them. How much she wanted to know him, in every possible way. Surely that said things about her she didn't want to acknowledge.

She had betrayed herself completely. She had tarnished Jeanette's memory. Sarina already knew that. What she couldn't understand was why she… kept right on going.

It was possible some part of her believed that raising her babies alone was no more than she deserved for having been so deeply foolish as to let this man close to her in the first place.

But that didn't explain why she *longed* for him. Why she woke in the night, her cheeks wet and images of him so real in her head she had to turn the light on to make sure he wasn't there beside her.

"I'm not going to argue with you," Matteo said when the silence drew out long enough to become

its own weapon. "Though I think you will find that it will not be so easy to walk away from me this next time. You can do as you like. But my children will remain with me, Sarina. Believe this, if nothing else."

She wanted to argue with him, but her throat was too tight—as if he'd wrapped his hands around it. And maybe there was something wrong with her, because there was some part of her that wished he would. That wished he would just…touch her again. No matter what that looked like. No matter what it did to her.

He did not take her to a hotel. He did not take her home to her barely lived-in condo. They drove instead to an airfield, where Matteo clearly expected her to board his private plane, heading— wherever he wanted to go.

Sarina thought about pitching a fit out there on the tarmac, but to what end? There was no one there to help her. There was no one there at all, save more of Matteo's ever-present staff.

His staff, his steady glare, and her own bad decisions.

She had no choice but to board the plane, take the seat he pointed toward, and wait to see what happened next.

The answer was—nothing. They flew through the night, and if she expected there would be more

fighting and arguing, or any interaction at all, she was disappointed.

You are not disappointed, she lectured herself, because she shouldn't have been. *This is a reprieve.*

Matteo disappeared into one of the staterooms and didn't emerge again until the plane began its descent into what looked like a never-ending mountain range, stretching out in white-tipped splendor on all sides.

"Do I get to know where we're going?" Sarina asked when he took one of the seats near her for their landing. "Or is the mystery part of my punishment?"

Matteo took his time answering her. His gray eyes were darker than she had ever seen them and she told herself the only response she had to that was the disinterest she ought to have felt. That it did not in any way scrape around inside of her, then make her melt in places she should have remained strong.

"The San Giacomos do not merely own property in Venice," he told her, his tone cool. Aristocratic, even. "They also took possession of a monastery in the Dolomites many centuries ago. It is more properly a fortress, unreachable by any means other than a very strenuous, weeklong hike or a significantly more convenient helicopter. We will be boarding one shortly."

"You are locking me away, in other words."

He shrugged, though his eyes gleamed. "If you like."

"You do realize, of course, that every single person in that bar saw you with me. When it becomes clear I have disappeared off the face of the planet, you will be the first person they ask."

"First they will have to find me," Matteo replied, all silken intent and that impenetrable darkness in his gaze.

Sarina had no idea how to respond to that without screaming, so she kept her mouth shut. And wished her heart would stop catapulting itself against her ribs as if it, too, wanted to escape.

Once they landed, there was no point refusing to exit the plane into the thin, cold air that rushed down from the snowy heights and burrowed beneath her skin. Or refusing to board the helicopter that waited for them there on the otherwise-deserted airfield.

But when the helicopter lowered them down behind the high, medieval walls that were carved into the side of a mountain and resembled nothing so much as a spectacularly remote prison, she understood that she should have fought harder. Or at all.

Because there was nothing here. Nothing at all but her certain doom.

And the brooding man at her side who would make sure he led her there.

"Snap out of it," she muttered to herself, under her breath, as the sound of the rotors faded into the crystal blue sky.

If Matteo heard her, he gave no sign.

He started across the courtyard, headed toward the ancient building chopped into the rock. And once again, Sarina felt that she had no option but to follow him.

She didn't want to stand out in the elements, waiting for it to snow. Which seemed surprisingly likely this high up, despite the fact that it was supposed to be spring. She expected the inside of a monastery turned fortress to be decorated much like Alcatraz, so she wasn't prepared when Matteo pushed open the great doors, solid wood and reinforced iron, and led her inside.

Where everything was… Warm. Right.

Sumptuous, she would have said.

And there was no particular reason that comfortable furnishings and a cozy, welcoming feeling should have left her feeling so confused, except it was one more way he had pushed her off balance.

He led her down a hallway, then up a set of stairs. And everywhere they went there were lights flickering in sconces, making the old stone hallways gleam gold. There were rich, bright tapestries on the walls, thick rugs on the floors, and it made the place built out of remote stone—built

from fear of God or fear of invaders, or possibly both—seem inviting.

Especially when he brought her to a sprawling bedchamber set up in the center of the building, with a view out over the courtyard and down over the cliffs, on and on into the mountaintops forever. The windows were old and arched, suitable for men with bows and chain mail, to Sarina's mind. But there were lights on in the bedchamber and a fire crackling away on one wall. It felt almost...homey.

When she turned to face the man who had brought her here, it didn't help any. The look on his face was severe. Stern and intense.

And Sarina had told herself so many stories to explain her behavior. She had gone over it again and again, trying to make sense of it for herself.

But she still didn't understand why it was that Matteo Combe could simply look at her and make her feel far too many things, complicated and enduring, deep inside.

"It's very pretty," she said, only aware that she was whispering when she heard the faint touch of her voice come back at her from the stone walls. "But it's still a prison, no matter how pretty you make it."

"Perhaps you should consider it more of a retreat."

"Kidnaps don't tend to turn into retreats, as a rule. No matter how pleasant the surroundings."

"Kidnaps." His dark eyes moved over her, and it felt the way laughter might, if he was a different man. If they were different people standing here, high above the world. "I do not recall putting a bag over your head and tossing you in the boot of my car, Sarina. Nor do I recall you objecting to that car. Or my plane. Or, indeed, the helicopter we rode here in happy silence with no restraints or gags. Doesn't a kidnap generally involve coercion?"

She sniffed. "I feel coerced."

Matteo looked almost pitying. "I don't think so. You concealed your pregnancy from me, yet I discovered it, quite by accident. That is not coercion you feel. It is your conscience."

And the fact her stomach twisted at that, making her feel uncomfortably hot and a little too close to sick again, suggested to her that he was a little more on the nose than she wanted to admit.

"Congratulations," she said after a moment, when she thought she could sound less…rattled than she felt. "You've transported me across the world and made sure we are about as secluded as anyone could be. Now what?"

"I'm so glad you asked." And though Matteo stood in the door to the room, looking wholly at his ease, a kind of warning shivered all over Sarina. "You have taken it upon yourself to psychoanalyze me at length, Doctor. Allow me to return the favor."

"I am a trained psychiatrist," Sarina pointed out, and told herself it was for professional reasons that her heart picked up its beat. "You are not."

"I will muddle through somehow."

Matteo waited. Until her mind stopped reeling around in pure terror. He waited until she surrendered to that steady gray gaze of his, no matter how little she wanted to, and simply stood there in the center of the bedchamber. Staring back at him. Wishing she had the power to mute him from afar, or transport herself back to San Francisco, the better to avoid all this from the start.

A terrible sense of foreboding grew in her, more intense by the second. It washed over her like that cold mountain wind outside, slicing into her, burrowing beneath her skin.

Making her think she might never be warm again.

"You look as if I have asked you to face the guillotine," he said after a moment. "Calm yourself, please. I have no intention of taking your head off."

Sarina forced a smile. "Let's just say I doubt very much you want to psychoanalyze me to tell me how wonderful you think I am."

"I think that tells us both something about how you view your profession, does it not?" But that hard, determined look on his face shut down any response she might have made. "This is what I

know about you, Sarina. You talk a good game. You run around the world while you do it. But in the end, all you know how to do is grieve."

She paled straight through. She felt tectonic plates shift and buckle, and thought she ought to dive for cover, but she could see that Matteo didn't move.

Which meant it was happening inside her.

She was the thing that was breaking apart, right here where she stood.

"What would happen," Matteo asked in an idle voice that was at complete odds with the intent look on his face, his dark gaze that same wild storm that had always been her undoing, "if you decided to live instead?"

CHAPTER ELEVEN

Matteo had not intended to bring Sarina here.

The monastery was a gift. A special place for family only that the San Giacomos had never shared with the outside world after its last days as a fortress against some long-ago war.

He had intended to take her back to Venice. To bring her full circle, and see where they ended up. He'd entertained several dark ideas as they'd driven through the streets of San Francisco.

He had boarded his plane in a cold fury, then taken himself off, because he was afraid that if he stayed in close proximity to her, he would succumb to the lure of her body. And if he succumbed to her, he suspected it was entirely possible he would take the edge off that fury in him. Matteo had not wanted soothe himself in any way.

He wanted to nurse it, he had realized an hour into the flight, when he had done nothing but pace in the confines of his stateroom at the back of the

jet, brooding over all the ways Sarina could have continued to deceive him well into her pregnancy. Well into his children's lives, in fact.

Would he ever have known about the babies she carried if he hadn't run into her?

He could feel that rage in him. It was like a fire, flames leaping and smoke billowing, and it would have been the easiest thing in the world to simply throw himself into it. To make himself a factory of his own fury, the way all his Combe ancestors had done, one after the next.

If he thought about it, it was the only thing he really knew how to do.

Here within these cold stone walls high in the Dolomites, warmed by a too-cheery fire and ancient tapestries, Sarina only gazed back at him. Her dark eyes were troubled and her cheeks were pale, as well they should be.

And she didn't answer his question.

"I wanted to make you pay," he told her, and the words felt as heavy as the stone walls all around them. The mountains looming above them. "You have wronged me and there should be a price for that. That was the way I was raised."

She blinked, and her lush, wide mouth twisted slightly. "I think many people would consider being stranded on the top of a mountain in the middle of nowhere, with no way out that doesn't

involve a helicopter or a Sherpa, an extreme consequence in and of itself."

But he noticed that she didn't sound as brash
and sure of herself as she had before. He had seen
the way his words had rocked her, and unless he
missed his guess, she was still reeling. Still trying to find her feet.

He was enough of his father's son to use that.

To use any means necessary.

"When I list all my sins and try on my own personal hair shirt, it always comes back to the same
choice," he said. It was what he had returned to
again and again during the long flight, first over
the great North American continent, then across
the Atlantic Ocean, all of it dark and fathomless
beneath the clouds. "I have told you more than
anyone need know about my father. But on the
other side of that equation there was my mother.
She either fought back in the same way, with desperate, drunken scenes, dramatics and fireworks.
Or she checked out."

"You mean...she left? Or she drank?"

Matteo's felt his expression turn harsh. "They
both drank. The drinking made them loud and
unpredictable. When my mother checked out, she
went quiet. It was as if she wrapped herself in gray
and disappeared." He remembered Alexandrina
that way, wrapped in blankets on her selection of
chaises, gazing steadily at nothing. Not respond-

ing. Not reacting. Not really there at all. "And I will never know if she did it because it infuriated my father or if it was the only way she could escape him."

"Are you angry for your father or for you?"

"I'm angry *at* me," he told her, and the sheer honesty of that shook through him. "I thought there would be time. That they would grow old and I would have years and years to figure them out. To understand why they did the things they did. And I never will. They will keep their secrets and their mysteries and I will never know if my mother checked out because she hated my father...or me."

Sarina said his name, soundlessly.

But he shook his head. "It doesn't matter, I suppose. My choices were clear to me from a young age. Engage violently. Or disappear. Guess which one I chose?"

Sarina swallowed hard at that, as if she was still fighting to keep her balance. As if the stone floors of this monastery pitched and rolled beneath her feet. After a beat or two, one delicate hand rose to her throat and she pressed her fingers against the very pulse point that told him truths about her he suspected she would rather keep to herself.

But he had every intention of using that, too.

"You are not required to act like either one of your parents, Matteo," she said into the quiet, and

her voice was so soft. So lacking its usual bite that it nearly gave him pause.

Nearly.

"My whole life I have prided myself on feeling nothing," Matteo told her, dark and sure now. He could feel the shift in him. As if he had spent his whole life blind, but now could see. And what he saw was Sarina. "Human emotion has always been a great mystery to me. I have had it shouted at me. I have lived in houses filled with it. But I have never understood its power, so I turned it off years ago. Or thought I did."

Her eyes looked too bright, but she stood straighter. "If this is your way of letting me know that it hurt your feelings that I didn't tell you I was pregnant—"

"I run my family's business. The only reason you know me at all is because I chose to involve myself in my sister's personal life. At my own father's funeral. We are standing in a former monastery where one of my ancestors copied sacred texts onto parchment. I am neck deep in family no matter what I do or where I go. It is the whole of my life."

"Matteo."

But he ignored the way she said his name. "You chose to keep it from me that I am soon to become a father, Sarina. That I will have my own

children. And yes, it turns out I have some feelings about that."

She breathed out, a ragged sound. And Matteo reminded himself that this wasn't what he wanted. He hadn't come here to fight with her. He was done with that.

He had watched this same cycle a thousand times. More. Nothing ever changed. Nothing was ever better; it was just the same roller coaster running over the same tracks, going nowhere.

"Matteo," she said again. "I know you think—"

But he held up a hand. And she surprised him by stopping.

"I already know how this goes," he said, low and dark. "You will talk about blackmail. I will talk about your agenda going into our sessions in the first place. I will talk about your pregnancy." He nodded at her belly and the children—*his children*—she carried. The future. Untouched by all these centuries of schemers and brawlers. Unmarked by the ghosts of the past. "And you will tell me that you don't know whether you would have told me eventually or not, but then again, neither do I. We can fight it out, again and again, until the babies you carry are full grown adults and have turned out just like us. Is that what you want?"

She had never looked more beautiful to him than she did now, literally blooming before him,

vibrant and real. Not a ghost. Not a memory he used to torture himself.

Flesh and blood and *right here.*

"Do I have a choice?" she fired back at him, though her voice was husky. "You already told me you will never forgive me. I don't suppose that matters, really. Unless what you mean by that is that you plan to thunder and snipe at me every time we meet."

"Every time we meet?" he repeated, as if he couldn't comprehend the words.

She made a jerky sort of gesture with one hand. "However it works. Custody agreements. Weekends here or there. I assume there are meetings involved, at some point or another."

Matteo had recognized something crucially important on that flight. What he'd taken for fury, that bright, red-hot current that had nearly bowled him over in that San Francisco bar, wasn't fury at all. Or it wasn't only fury.

It was braided through with far more complicated emotions than that.

Fear, for one, that he was doomed to repeat the mistakes every last one of his ancestors—and particularly his parents—had made. A kind of mad desire to get his hands on her, anyway he could. To touch her. Explore her. Only partly because his children grew inside of her.

And underneath all of that, more terrifying and deeper by far, a fierce and comprehensive joy.

"What if I told you that custody agreements and the odd weekend aren't what I want?" he asked, his voice more of a growl.

Sarina stiffened. Her hands sneaked over her belly, as if she was warding him off. As if she thought she needed to protect herself from him—and that, too, was familiar. It reminded him of entirely too many nights in his own childhood. Too many rooms heavy with tension and the remnants of the terrible things his parents shouted at each other.

Matteo refused to believe he was doomed to repeat these same dire histories, over and over again.

"If you think that you can take these babies from me, think again," Sarina shot at him. "I'll fight you tooth and nail."

Matteo moved all the way into the room at that, his gaze fast on hers, his heart thundering in his chest.

"I have spent all these months in hotel rooms. Jet-lagged and alone, up at odd hours in strange cities. And the only constant was you."

She started at that, her lips parting as if she meant to say something. Or fight, then and there. But she didn't.

He reached over and touched her, running his hand over the smooth ink of her hair, because she was there. Because this was real.

Because he was done with ghosts.

"You haunted me, Sarina. Everywhere I went, everything I did, there you were."

"You must have nights like that all the time," she said, and though her words were bold and dismissive, he could see the sheen of vulnerability in her gaze.

"Do you?" he countered.

He fit his hand to the side of her face, holding her there. And for a moment, he felt her melt. She even leaned into his hand.

One breath, then another, and it felt like a gift.

It told him that he hadn't created his own phantoms, out there in all those hotel rooms that blurred together in his mind. He hadn't imagined the way they fit.

Or the way she felt.

"Here's the trouble," she said quietly, and then stepped back. "I just don't believe you." She shook her head when he opened his mouth. "You're the man who has a video recording of me. Who had every intention of releasing it unless I did what you wanted. And I did, but there's nothing to prevent you from releasing it when you see fit. And please don't tell me that it's been deleted. We live in a distressingly digital world, Matteo. Nothing's ever really deleted, is it?"

"Surely when you have my babies it might be a clue that our relationship is not strictly profes-

sional, no?" he asked, dryly. "I am not certain why it would matter if it was released at this point. Though it will not be."

"You took such care to make sure that you recorded me in your office. It undercuts my professional reputation and you know it. And you have it. And I can't convince myself that this..." And as she looked around the room, he saw even more of that vulnerability in her gaze. It kicked at him like his own heart. "A fancy fortress hidden away in the mountains, furnished like a fairy tale, isn't just another way for you to manipulate me into giving you what you want."

He fought the urge in him to put his hands on her again. To remind her that if he wanted to manipulate her, he had far more effective weapons in his arsenal. "What is it you think I want?"

"Heirs," she said immediately, as if that was a curse. "I think you want your heirs. Both of your family lines have been obsessed with their bloodlines since the dawn of time. I think you spent that entire plane ride figuring out how best to maneuver me into handing them over to you so you can make them just like you. However possible."

"You don't have to hand them over to anyone." Matteo watched her face closely, ignoring the tightness in his chest. "I want to marry you, Sarina."

And the bitter laugh she let out at that was not exactly what he had been going for.

"I bet you do. Wouldn't that be a feather in your cap. Not only do you marry the woman who tried to take you down—which would also, of course, call into question my assessment of you and potentially ruin me. But you also get to make your children legitimate, which everyone knows is what people like you live for."

He watched her closely, watching that vulnerability on her face shift to something more like panic when he didn't rage back at her.

"Let us put this into terms you understand, little one," he said. "Give me your mobile phone."

Sarina frowned at him, every inch of her suspicious. And he supposed there was something wrong with him, that he should find that so endearing. Even when all that suspicion was aimed at him.

"So you can sling it off a battlement and watch it splinter to a thousand pieces below?" she demanded. "Why would I do that?"

"Your mobile, Sarina."

There was a mulish set to her jaw as she dug into her pocket, pulled it out, then handed it over.

Matteo fiddled with the mobile for a moment, then handed back to her.

"Point that at me," he ordered her. "It is already filming."

She stared at him, then down at the phone in her hand. Then back at him. Though he noticed she also lifted the mobile as she did it, pointing its camera straight at him.

"I did not spend that long plane ride thinking of ways to manipulate you," he told her, grave and certain. As certain as the stones all around them. "I thought instead about what it is I want."

"You say that as if those are two separate things."

"My family's legacy means something to me, I won't deny it. But so much of that legacy is bound up in *things*. A company with offices across the globe. Pretty houses and villas and once upon a time monasteries all over Europe, cluttered up with the ghosts of the past. But there is a difference between a living legacy and a collection of monuments."

"I assumed that for families like yours it was all the same."

He did not take the defiant tilt of her chin personally, nor the way her free hand curled into a fist. He told himself he wasn't the only one in this room with ghosts.

"My parents' marriage was entirely about the past," he said, and he knew it was true. It was what made it so hard to grieve them. And what had made it difficult to be around them while they'd lived. "There was no forgiveness for mistakes

made. There was no future. They returned, over and over and over again, to old slights. Ancient betrayals. Theirs was a marriage entirely based on all the ways they had failed each other from the start."

He wanted to touch her again, but he didn't. He had to take notice of the way her hand shook as it held up that mobile phone. He had to look for meaning in the way her cheeks bloomed with heat.

He had to believe in this. In her. In them.

"You are pregnant with my children," he said, his voice intense but no match for the wildfire inside of him. "You will make me a father. And I am a man who has spent an entire lifetime trying his best to be nothing at all like mine. And yet even so, my first knee-jerk reaction to discovering your pregnancy was temper. And you're right, I wanted to hurt you in return. But Sarina. Hear this, if nothing else. I don't want to be that man."

"Why are you doing this?" she asked, her voice a whisper again, and he didn't know if she meant the recording she was making. Or the fact that they were here, so far away from the world and everything in it. But it didn't matter.

Because Matteo, who had spent a lifetime determined never, ever to surrender to another living soul, or feel a damned thing, sank down on his knees before her.

Like a flesh and blood man taken over by his heart.

"You have haunted me since the day I met you," he told her, holding her gaze with his the way he wanted to hold her. "One night was not enough and could never be enough. I think I'm in love with you. I hear your voice in my head. I wake from dreams about you every night, then lie awake, reliving every moment we spent together in my head."

"Obsession is not the same as love," she hissed at him.

"It seems to me we have a good six months to figure that out." He lifted his hands toward her, and kept them there, a kind of supplication. Or perhaps it was a prayer. "I don't want to marry you because you're pregnant, Sarina. Though that makes it sweeter. You challenge me. You fascinate me. You're not afraid of me. I have spent months trying to tell myself that your effect on me will fade. That I will forget you in time. But I do not believe I ever will. Did you think I ended up in San Francisco by chance? I wanted to find you."

"You blackmailed me," she threw at him. "And you've followed that up with abducting me. Where exactly do you think this relationship is going?"

"I don't know," he said simply. "I never thought I could feel a thing. Now all I do is feel."

She made a noise at that, but Matteo wasn't finished.

"When my mother died, I refused to let it reg-

ister. She was always so distant. So disengaged. I told myself I didn't care, because I didn't *want* to care. But now, thanks to you, I find myself wondering if that was just a lie I told myself. And if she was the problem all these years—or if I was. I am not certain she could help her moods, but I know I could. I chose to be the way I was. And I don't have the slightest idea how to be a better man, Sarina. I never have. But I want to try." His hands were still outstretched between them and he didn't know if he wanted her to take them, or if he wanted to touch her. Only that he wanted her. "Will you try with me?"

And he saw it then. Moisture making tracks down her cheeks. She dropped the hand holding her mobile to her side, and he had never seen the expression he saw on her face then.

Almost as if she was…defeated.

But this was Sarina. The toughest challenge he'd ever faced.

Still, her voice was small when she answered, and it made him ache. Everywhere.

"I've tried," she whispered. "I really have, Matteo. But I don't know how."

CHAPTER TWELVE

"I DON'T KNOW how to do anything but grieve," Sarina said, repeating those words Matteo had said to her that she was surprised hadn't ripped her wide-open. "You said so yourself and you weren't wrong."

And she could hear the anguish in her own voice.

She could feel it, everywhere, the way she had for years now. The way she always did and had long understood she always would.

Matteo still knelt there before her, proud and beautiful, and whatever earthquake had wrecked her before kept going. Shaking her over and over, until she wasn't sure what was left of her. Or who she was meant to be in the aftermath.

"You loved your friend," Matteo said softly, with what looked like kindness in those storm-colored eyes of his. She wasn't sure she could bear it. "You called her your sister. Do you really think she would begrudge it if you moved on?"

And Sarina let out a sound then. It wasn't a

laugh, because it was too dark, too filled with regret for that. Maybe it was a sob, torn out from somewhere deep inside.

She wasn't sure she could tell the difference any longer.

"You have held on to her memory for all this time." Matteo sounded as if he was trying to soothe her. And there was a treacherous kind of softening, deep within her, that made her imagine he could. If she let him. "You have honored her in every possible way. Surely it's time to do something other than grieve."

"I was so angry with her."

It took Sarina a moment to realize that she was the one who had spoken. That those words were out there now, the deepest, darkest secret she carried inside of her. Those words that were like scar tissue. Disfiguring her, deep inside. And never fading entirely, no matter what.

She had never said them out loud before.

And now she had, she felt…outside herself. Unmoored.

And as if she had betrayed Jeanette all over again.

"I was never nice about that man," she told Matteo now, because his gray gaze was steady and the words seemed to pour out of her as if he'd called them forth. "I hated him from day one. And I wasn't shy about letting her know. I thought she was

an idiot to imagine he would ever want that baby and believe me, I told her so. And when she called me, sobbing and in tears from that hotel suite, I tried to be supportive. He had done something so awful to her. Unimaginably vile. I hated him even more." She felt that sobbing thing again, like its own storm lodged deep inside of her. And now, horribly, breaking free. "But what did she expect?"

She shook her head at the sound of that question, her voice cracking as she asked it. The way it always did. The way it had. Images of that morning flooded through her the way they always did, reminding her of who she was.

Exactly who she was.

"Do I seem like a good friend to you, Matteo? A decent sister? Because I'm not." She shook her head. "I'm the one who fought with the closest person to me in all the world when what she needed was my love and understanding. She was miscarrying and I was furious with her. That's who I am."

"What did you expect?" She'd shouted that exact question at Jeanette in the car on the way back home from the hotel. "What did you *think* would happen?"

"Not this!" Jeanette had screamed right back.

Because they had been the kind of close that came with constant explosions mixed in with all that laughter. Silent treatments that lasted weeks, then ended with a shrug and too much sugar. A

harsh word instead of a hug, which they'd called *honesty*. They had prided themselves on the way they'd cut into each other.

Family, they'd called themselves. Though neither of their families had ever screamed at them the way they did at each other, as that would have required noticing they existed. They'd wallowed in their emotions. All of their emotions. When they weren't fighting, they considered those emotions their greatest strength.

"I thought he loved me," Jeanette had cried. "He did love me. I know he did."

"He never loved you, Jeanette," Sarina had snapped. "He used you. That's what men like him do."

"You don't know him!" Jeanette had thrown at her. There in Sarina's car while she sat on a stolen hotel towel and lost the baby she'd carried. "If you weren't so obsessed with studying all the time, maybe you'd fall in love. Maybe then you'd be a little bit less self-righteous."

"I'm sorry this is happening to you," Sarina had thrown right back at her friend. Her sister. "But I told you it would. From the very start, I told you—"

"It must be wonderful to be so perfect, Sarina," Jeanette had sneered at her. "You must be so *proud*."

And it had gotten much worse from there.

"She needed help," Sarina told Matteo now.

"And I gave her a stern talking-to instead, as if that could change what was done to her. And then in the morning, she was gone. And I get to spend the rest of my life living with the fact that when she needed me the most, I decided that what she *really* needed was to face up to reality."

Matteo didn't look at her as if she was a monster, and that made it worse.

"You couldn't have known," he said.

"Do you want to know the sick truth?" Sarina moved closer to him, jabbing furiously at the wetness on her cheeks that blurred her eyes, as well. "I've spent years sitting with guilt. But I didn't really understand her. I thought she was weak. I felt guilty because I kicked her when she was already down, but the truth—the real truth—is that I thought she couldn't help it. She acted as if she had no power over the things that happened to her. And I was sure that I was different. That I would never, ever compromise myself to be with anyone. And then I met you."

If anything, Matteo seemed more beautiful now. More compelling, more impossibly magnetic, even though she knew exactly how dangerous he was to her.

And worse, how deeply she would betray herself—and had—just to touch him.

"And look at me now." Sarina let out a hollow sort of laugh, ignoring that same expression

on his face. As if he understood, when she knew he couldn't. Of course he couldn't. She had never been able to understand it herself. "I've compromised myself in every possible way and there's no excuse for it. I slept with you when I was meant to be assessing you, and I can talk about gray areas and who my real client was until I'm blue in the face, but we both know I crossed the line. And I can't even pretend that you're the one who did it. I crossed that line all by myself. I leaped across it, brandishing my virginity like a prize."

"That is not quite how I recall it," Matteo said, in a soft way with a hint of laughter that only made all that darkness inside her worse.

Because she didn't deserve laughter. Or softness. She knew she never would.

"I slept with you. I let you blackmail me. I lied to your entire board of directors because you asked me to. And when I found out I was pregnant, my first thought wasn't how I got myself into such a mess. My first thought was a sick kind of delight that someday, somewhere, I knew that the fact I was having your babies meant I would see you again." Sarina thought she was going to laugh again, but this time there was no denying that what came out was a sob. "All Jeanette did was fall in love. I don't have the slightest idea why I did any of the things I've done. What would make a per-

son act like that? Like this. What could possibly compel—"

"This, little one." Matteo reached out, taking a firm grip of her arms and pulling her to him. "This."

She sank down to her knees, too, so she was facing him as he brought her into the circle of his strong arms. And she shuddered when she saw the expression in his dark gray eyes, up close so there could be no mistake.

Tender.

And worse still, sure.

"I don't want this," she whispered. "I never wanted this."

Matteo's beautiful mouth curved. "Too bad."

And then he set his mouth to hers.

It was a kiss. A claiming. It was gentle and sweet, and it filled her with light. It was hope and it was joy, and she didn't know what to do about any of those things except to lean into him. Kiss him back.

Melt against him, the way she had from the start.

"Marry me," he said against her mouth. "Fight with me if you like, Doctor. Just promise me you will do it forever."

And he left her mouth, raining kisses all over her face. He lifted her up to her feet before him, but kept his hands at her hips. Holding her steady, she understood. Propping her up when her own legs felt rubbery beneath her.

"Marry me," he said again. And again.

And then he pushed up her shirt, exposing her belly. Then set his mouth to her navel, laying kisses all around that soft swell that held their future.

"I don't know how to do this," Sarina sobbed at him.

"I think you do."

And he kissed her. He soothed her.

It felt new. Huge and impossible, but if she leaned into it, it was nothing short of glorious.

She didn't know who started removing clothes, but all that soothing turned to flame. And that flame began to dance, higher and higher.

And then it seemed she couldn't help herself. She needed to be naked. She needed him to be naked, too.

They had been together so briefly and apart too long. And Sarina couldn't stand another moment without him,

The first time she took him, there on the floor on the soft rug. She climbed over him, settled herself upon him, and took him deep inside of her.

"This is what forever feels like," he told her.

That deep, slick slide. His hardness and her softness, and all that melting that made them one.

Matteo's hands were on her hips. His gaze was locked to hers.

And they fell off the side of the world together.

She was still spinning when he picked her up,

carrying her from the floor to the bed, then curling himself around her.

"The only forever I know is a revenge fantasy," she confessed.

He brushed her hair back from her face, smiling at her as if she was beautiful. As if she was good.

And when he looked at her that way, she felt as if she could be.

"We can play out any fantasies you like, little one," he promised her. "You think this kind of chemistry comes along every day?"

And it shouldn't have been possible to feel that fire again, but she did. And she knew he did, too, because his grin was wolfish as he tipped her over onto her back, pulled her knees up high, then settled himself between them.

"Marry me," he said again.

And then he began to tease her.

He held her down, and set his mouth to every single part of her body. He made her writhe, then sob. He brought her close, time and again, but then retreated.

"Marry me," he demanded, when she was making keening sounds, her head thrashing back and forth on the pillows.

"All right," she finally cried, breaking. Because she couldn't remember why she shouldn't. Not when the world had disappeared, leaving nothing at all but him. "I'll marry you."

And only then did he surge inside her at last.

She exploded at once, crying out in some mad combination of joy and hope, and a thousand other things she hardly dared name.

He pounded into her, murmuring love words in every language he knew, and she didn't have to understand the words to thrill to them each time.

He built up that fire in her all over again, and when she broke yet again, he came with her.

His gaze was like silver, bright with the happiness Sarina could feel inside her, too.

"Remember this," Matteo told her, holding her as if she was precious, so high above the world, surrounded by stone and certainty, and his arms like both. "This is how it's going to feel, Sarina. Always and forever, just like this."

And it did.

Ten years later, Sarina kissed each one of her nine-year-old twin boys goodbye, peeked in on the six-year-old who was teaching herself to read in her bed, and assured herself that the toddler was fast asleep. Then she left them all in the extremely capable hands of their battalion of certified nannies, and joined her husband on the roof of the ancient San Giacomo villa in Venice.

"Consider this an abduction," Matteo said, his gray eyes alight with a dark storm of passion that was only hers, mixed in with the gleaming silver

that was theirs. They made it together, each and every day.

Every laugh. Every touch. Every secret smile.

"I do love an abduction," she said with a laugh. "Happy anniversary, my love."

He kissed her there, on the rooftop of the place where they had first met. With that same fire. That endless need.

The glory that was all theirs. Still.

Matteo helped her board the helicopter that waited for them. And as it rose into the Venetian night, then flew north, Sarina reflected on the past decade.

It was so hard to remember who she had been, back then.

That woman so afraid to love. So certain that it would all end, and badly. So convinced that because her friend had been unhappy, and they had both been so immature, she deserved nothing but pain.

It had taken years to undo those knots, but she'd done it. She and Matteo had followed each thread and pulled them straight, one after the next. In both of them.

They had stayed in the monastery for weeks, emerging only to attend to matters that truly couldn't be missed. They had gotten to know each other without angry board members, agendas, or the outside world.

But she hadn't married him until she was eight

months pregnant, so huge that all she could do was waddle, wondering if she would survive giving birth to the two baby boys inside of her.

"Marry me," he said, one bright day in London. "Or are you waiting so that our children can walk you down the aisle?"

She had her father walk her down the aisle, there in the gardens of Combe Manor. She thought they'd reclaimed it that day, taking it back from the ghosts, and setting it up for their future.

And that night, she lay with Matteo in that same bed in that master suite where she'd lost her heart so completely. Over and over again.

Except this time, she'd known what it was that she felt when she was with him.

"I love you," she whispered.

He grinned at her, brushing her hair back from her face so he could gaze into her eyes.

Her husband. Her life.

"I am well aware, little one," he told her.

"I love you," she said again, relishing the words on her tongue. "And I think I love you even more for marrying me without making me say it."

"You would never believe in love unless it came wrapped up tight with unbreakable vows," he said, already moving to set the hardest part of himself against her, right there where she yielded into softness and molten heat. "And I do not mind making vows to you, Sarina."

Because every vow they made to each other, they kept.

She gave birth to their twin sons and he was there to take each one in his arms, then smile at her as if she had remade the world.

He was there when their daughter came, angrier by far. And he was the one who suggested that they call her Jeanette, after the friend—the sister—that Sarina would never stop missing.

And he was by her side when their fourth baby came too quickly, giving them all a scare. He was her rock as they waited for news, and he dried her tears when all was well and their third son was finally placed in her arms.

That was what Matteo did. He showed up. He supported her.

Day after day, year after year, he taught her how to live.

In return she taught him that he had always been a man, human straight through, no matter how he pretended otherwise. And one after the next, they untied all their knots and vanquished all their ghosts, together.

Because the other side of grief was love.

She continued her practice, shifting away from the corporate clients to focus more on women in need of healing, not revenge. For his part, Matteo learned how to delegate, so that he need not be a janitor to his family—unless that was what he wanted.

And as the helicopter landed high up in the Dolomites, there in the courtyard of the fortress she would always consider the finest and sweetest retreat in all the world, Sarina reflected that it had been a long time indeed since she'd last thought of the things that had haunted them so much when they'd started.

"Why are you smiling?" Matteo asked, taking her hand as they walked across the courtyard and lacing their fingers tight together. The way he always did.

"I was just thinking," she replied. "I can't recall the last time we saw a ghost."

She was making a joke, but his expression turned serious. Those beloved gray eyes, stern and sure, lit up with all they'd done over these past ten years.

And the promise of what came next.

"Ghosts are of the past," he told her, rich and low, while the mountains stood as witness. "But you and I, Sarina. We have nothing ahead of us but the future, bright and clear."

And hand in hand, more in love than they'd been at the start, they found it.

Together.

* * * * *